"Out, Jessica. I'm fine.
I don't need your help."

Jessica was so taken aback by the sight of his naked torso that she almost obeyed without question. Those baggy shirts and sweaters had hidden muscular arms, a smooth, tan back and broad, powerful shoulders. Her mouth went dry. *That* was what she'd been sharing a camper with? A world-class hunk with the build of a professional athlete? Good grief!

She swallowed hard. "I'm not leaving until I check those cuts. Your macho orders don't impress me, and neither does your sarcasm. If you need to see a doctor, you're darn well going to see one, even if I have to help myself to your cycle and ride out to get him."

Griff turned around, giving Jessica her first good view of his chest. It more than matched the rest of him, especially in the rippling muscle department. Several fine scratches crisscrossed the flesh, oozing blood into the light scattering of hair.

"You're sure you're the same woman I interviewed last week?"

Dear Reader:

In May of 1980 Silhouette had a goal. We wanted to bring you the best that romance had to offer—heartwarming, poignant stories that would move you time and time again.

Mission impossible? Not likely, because in 1980 and all the way through to today, we have authors with the same dream we have—writers who strive to bring you stories with a distinctive medley of charm, wit, and above all, *romance*.

And this fall we're celebrating in the Silhouette Romance line—we're having a Homecoming! In September some of your all-time favorite authors are returning to their "alma mater." Then, during October, we're honored to present authors whose books always capture the magic—some of the wonderful writers who have helped maintain the heartwarming quality the Silhouette Romance line is famous for.

Come home to Romance this fall and for always. Help celebrate the special world of Silhouette Romance.

I hope you enjoy this book and the many books to come.

Sincerely,

Tara Hughes
Senior Editor
Silhouette Books

BROOKE HASTINGS

Too Close for Comfort

Silhouette *Romance*

Published by Silhouette Books New York

America's Publisher of Contemporary Romance

SILHOUETTE BOOKS
300 E. 42nd St., New York, N.Y. 10017

Copyright © 1987 by Deborah H. Gordon

ISBN: 0-373-08528-1

First Silhouette Books printing September 1987

America's Publisher of Contemporary Romance

Printed in the U.S.A.

Books by Brooke Hastings

Silhouette Romance

Playing for Keeps #13
Innocent Fire #26
Desert Fire #44
Island Conquest #67
Winner Take All #101
Too Close for Comfort #528

Silhouette Special Edition

Intimate Strangers #2
Rough Diamond #21
A Matter of Time #49
An Act of Love #79
Tell Me No Lies #156
Hard to Handle #250
As Time Goes By #294
Forward Pass #312
Double Jeopardy #349
Forbidden Fruit #385

Silhouette Intimate Moments

Interested Parties #37
Reasonable Doubts #64

BROOKE HASTINGS

is a transplanted Easterner who now lives in California with her husband and two children. A full-time writer, she won the Romance Writers of America's Golden Medallion Award for her Silhouette Romance, *Winner Take All*. She especially enjoys doing background research for her books, and finds it a real challenge to come up with new plot twists and unique characters for her stories.

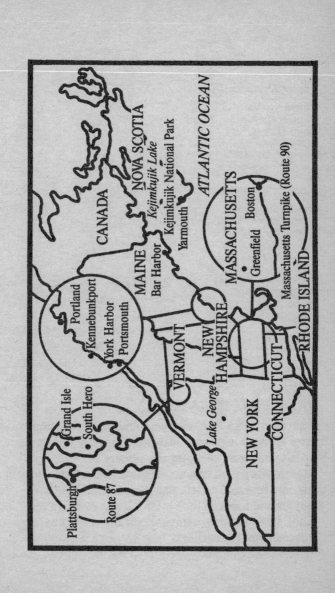

Chapter One

Arthur Griffin Marshall, Jr. regarded his buzzing telephone with a relief he had no business feeling. Every time he made up his mind to take a vacation, somebody came along with a case that was either too interesting or too lucrative to turn down. He'd been going along that way for four years now and had promised his family it wouldn't happen again, but a very large part of him was hoping that it would.

He picked up the phone and barked out an order before his secretary had a chance to get a word in. "Whoever it is, let Roxy handle it." Roxy—Roxanne Pascal—was his partner. "I was just about to leave."

His secretary paid him no attention. "It's Alex Ulanoff, Griff, and he asked to speak to you personally. I think you should take the call."

Griff frowned, trying to place the name. It only took a moment. Alex Ulanoff was the director of the New England Theater Company. He was in his late thirties, about to begin his fourth season with N.E.T.C., and by all accounts very successful. The son of Nicolai Ulanoff, the world-famous concert pianist, Alex had made a name for himself in Boston both as a fixture in high society and as a playwright and director.

Griff was almost intrigued enough to find out what Ulanoff wanted—almost, but not quite. "Tell him I'm going on vacation next week." His excuse met with such a long-suffering sigh from his secretary that he decided to throw himself on her mercy. "Damn it, Vicki, you've got to save me from my own worst instincts. My sister's nagging me, my mother's nagging me—even Roxy's nagging me. You're the only one who doesn't think I work too hard. I'm going fishing Monday even if it kills me."

Vicki sniffed that he'd probably die of boredom before overwork had a chance to do him in, and broke the connection. Griff assumed that would be the end of it, but twenty seconds later she was back on the line.

"Ulanoff says he knows your father from Harvard and that's why he called. He says it's a delicate matter and that he can't entrust it to just anyone." She paused, then asked slyly, "Don't you just love a good mystery?"

If Griff hadn't loved mysteries, he never would have become a private detective. Bowing to the inevitable, he mumbled that he would speak to Ulanoff after all and pressed down the lighted button on his phone.

"Griff Marshall, Mr. Ulanoff. I'll be on vacation for the next couple of weeks, but if your problem can wait that long, I'll be glad to talk to you about it when I get back."

"On the contrary," Ulanoff said, "your vacation couldn't come at a better time, at least as far as my problem is concerned. Her name is Jessica Lawrence and I want her to disappear for the next month or so—until August fifteenth, to be precise. How does twenty-five hundred a week plus expenses strike you?"

"For kidnapping somebody?" Griff told himself the man had to be joking. "I have an aversion to breaking the law, Mr. Ulanoff, but if you wanted to grab my attention you've succeeded. Go on."

Ulanoff laughed. "Guilty as charged, I'm afraid. I suppose it's the playwright in me." He cleared his throat. "From what I've heard about the work you've done in the past, my problem is outside your usual area of specialization. I decided to contact you because your father is my colleague at Harvard. No son of Arthur G. Marshall could possibly be anything but intelligent and cultured, and that's why you're so perfect for the job. Jessica happens to be very precious to me, Mr. Marshall. I love her and I intend to marry her. At the moment she's caught in the middle of a violent quarrel about the future of the family company, and it's tearing her apart. If I remove her from the scene, they'll have to make a decision without her. It's that simple."

Maybe to Alex Ulanoff, but not to Griff Marshall. A former FBI agent, Griff wasn't about to kidnap anybody—not even for her own good. "The answer still has to be no," he said. "Why don't you take her to Europe for the summer if you want to get her out of the way?"

"I wish I could, but I have a play to finish writing, money to raise for next season, and rehearsals to conduct." Ulanoff added that kidnapping wasn't really what he had in mind; it was more in the nature of baby-sitting. He explained that he'd already suggested to Jessica that she take an out-of-town job for the summer and she'd agreed it was a good idea, but that she'd never been on her own before. He was concerned about how she would get along and wanted Griff to look after her.

"Without her knowing it, you mean," Griff said.

"Exactly. She's got some crazy idea about needing to become more independent and she refuses to let me arrange something with one of my friends. She'd be furious if she knew I was doing it behind her back, but I don't see any alternative. Jessica's family has always coddled and protected her. She's a classical music student and she lives in her own private world. She's not equipped to handle her own money or run her own life. Frankly, it scares the hell out of me to think of her working for slave wages at some summer resort, which is what she has in mind. She's too inexperienced and naive."

Griff was beginning to get the picture. Still, he wanted more information before he committed himself one way or the other. Ulanoff wasn't hesitant about supplying it, explaining that Jessica Lawrence had been adopted by her paternal grandparents after her parents were killed in an accident. Everyone in the family had pitched in to raise her—not only her grandparents, Henry and Ethel Lawrence, but also her two uncles, Ernest and Charles.

"Ethel died eight months ago and Henry four months after that," Ulanoff told Griff. "The old man owned exactly seventy-eight percent of the stock in the family company, Lawrence Shoes, with the rest of it held by dozens of different relatives and retired employees. When Henry died, his stock was split into three equal portions—twenty-six percent to each of his two surviving sons, Ernest and Charles, and to Jessica. The two men have been arguing ever since about whether to stay in business. Lawrence Shoes is a solid enough firm, but it's too small to compete effectively with the real giants in the business. Charles wants to sell the company to a conglomerate—take the money and invest it elsewhere—and Ernest wants to exercise an option his father negotiated shortly before his death to purchase another shoe company and expand into the national market. Both of them are pressuring Jessica to vote their way. Either choice makes sense financially, so the two men have made it into a test of her love and loyalty. I'm sure you can appreciate how impossible it would be for her to choose between the two of them when both have been equally good to her."

"And what happens August fifteenth?" Griff asked, referring to the date Ulanoff had mentioned in the beginning of their conversation.

"Both the option to buy the other shoe company and the offer from the conglomerate will expire. Lawrence Shoes holds its annual meeting on the fifteenth, so the matter will be settled one way or the other at that time."

"And if Jessica isn't available, Charles and Ernest will be forced to turn to the minor stockholders to try to get the votes they need to win."

"That's right," Ulanoff said. "When all is said and done, both men are realists. Let's assume Jessica leaves town without telling them where she's going. Obviously they would do their best to track her down, but if they can't find her they'll accept the fact that she's out of the picture and focus their efforts on the minor stockholders. That's where you come in. I've given the matter a great deal of thought, and I believe I've come up with a way to reconcile Jessica's desire for independence with my own need to know she's safe. I'm sure a man of your talents will be able to pull it off."

Griff had a bemused look on his face when he hung up the phone ten minutes later. Ulanoff was probably a very good playwright, because he certainly had a good imagination. Griff had stalled about giving him a final answer, but still, it was going to be hard to turn down two-and-a-half grand a week for a job that was more or less a paid vacation. Jes-

sica Lawrence was apparently as timid as she was un-
worldly. How much trouble could she be?

He and Roxy never took a case without consulting each
other first, so he went next door to fill her in. She listened
with a gradually widening smile, finally teasing, "Some guys
have all the luck. Are you sure you don't want to stick with
your fishing and let me handle this one?"

Roxanne Pascal was a divorced single parent in her early
thirties with a talent for playing a variety of different roles.
She'd carried off some crazy assignments in her time, but
some things were beyond even her abilities. "Sorry, Roxy,"
Griff said. "You would never pass the physical."

"Neither would you." She looked him up and down,
leering a little in appreciation. Most women liked what they
saw when Griff walked by, a fact he'd taken full advantage
of. It wasn't so much that he'd had a lot of women as that
he'd had most of the ones he'd really wanted. He was
choosy, but he could well afford to be.

"You'll have to do your Clark Kent number," Roxy went
on. "One look at you and the poor girl will probably run as
fast as she can in the opposite direction."

The reference to Clark Kent was a standing joke between
the two of them. Unlike most of his fellow agents at the FBI,
Griff hadn't been an attorney or an accountant. He'd been
hired because of his talent for math and computer science,
and assigned to track down everything from teenage hack-
ers out for a little fun to white-collar programming experts
trying to embezzle millions.

Four years with the bureau had taught him he wasn't cut
out to function in a bureaucracy, so he'd resigned as an
agent and gone into business for himself. His specialties
were industrial espionage and computer fraud, and his cases
usually involved undercover work at high-tech firms. His
appearance had presented a bit of a problem—he looked

more like a jock than a math nerd—but a little creativity had solved it. He'd started with a pair of huge, thick-lensed glasses and an appallingly bad haircut, then added a wardrobe full of the worst polyester abominations in the entire Boston area. The pièces de résistance had been the distracted air he'd managed to affect and the really awful jokes he'd constantly told. In four years of cases, nobody had ever guessed that he wasn't the oddball new employee he typically pretended to be.

Jessica Lawrence was going to require a slightly different approach, but Griff had never been short on confidence. She would believe exactly what he wanted her to believe and go on believing it until the day she died, unless Alex Ulanoff saw fit to tell her otherwise. Griff was convinced he could talk his way in or out of anything, so a naive little student with her head in the clouds wasn't going to cause him much concern.

"I've decided to think of it as a new and higher challenge," he told Roxy. "Clark Kent, twenty-four hours a day instead of only eight. What do you suppose he sleeps in? Permanent press pajamas?"

"Don't forget the satin robe and the leather slippers." Roxy lazed back in her chair. "You're going to take the case, I assume?"

"Probably. I told Ulanoff I'd get back to him tonight or tomorrow morning. I want to check him out with my father first and then see what I can find out about the Lawrence Shoe Company and the New England Theater Company."

"You don't trust him?" Roxy looked a little surprised.

"Would you?" Griff asked. "The guy offered me two-and-a-half-grand a week. You don't earn that kind of money directing a nonprofit theater company or teaching a few courses at Harvard."

Roxy nodded, silently conceding the point. Then, good soldier that she was, she offered to help him with his phone calls. Griff was good at getting people to talk, but not as good as Roxy. When she turned on the sugar and spice, the most amazing confidences flowed from the other end of the line.

As he got up to leave, he told himself the gods had been smiling on him the day she'd walked through his door to apply for a job as his secretary. It hadn't taken him long to spot her potential and send her for some additional training. Promoting her to his associate had been the best move he'd ever made. There was nothing romantic about his feelings for her, but if he ever *did* fall in love, it was going to be with a woman who was every bit as clever, independent and confident as Roxy Pascal was.

Chapter Two

Jessica Lawrence pushed the collar of her raincoat up around her ears as she emerged from the M.T.A. and dashed toward Harvard Yard. She was nervous, she was running late, and now it had started pouring to beat the band. By the time she got to Professor Marshall's office, she was going to look like a drowned rat. So much for the crisp, capable image she'd meant to project.

She felt such a sharp stab of doubt when she came to Marshall's building that she almost turned around and left. She wasn't qualified for this job. She never should have answered the ad. She wouldn't last five minutes before Marshall found out what a fraud she was and sent her packing.

On the other hand, he'd listed very few specific requirements and she met them all perfectly. She stopped just inside the doorway and recited the ad in her head, trying to convince herself she wouldn't be wasting his time. *Wanted: Recent college graduate to assist prominent sociologist in summer field study. Honor student preferred. Must be free*

to travel extensively. The ad hadn't said anything about
wanting a sociology major; it had simply directed interested applicants to send a resumé to a post office box in
Cambridge. Jessica had mailed in her answer the same day
the ad had appeared.

She hadn't expected anything to come of it, but Dr. Marshall's secretary had phoned her only two days later to set
up an interview. Jessica was surprised when the woman
mentioned who her boss was, and then a little intimidated.
She'd taken only one sociology course in college, a survey
of the most important work in the field, but even she recognized the name Arthur G. Marshall. The class had read
excerpts from his most recent book, an analysis of the dif-
fering organizational styles of the army, navy and air force
and the problems those differences created when the three
branches of the military tried to work together. Obviously
Marshall was a brilliant man, probably the type who
expected and got perfection from his assistants.

She took a deep breath and started down the hall, wishing she had time to stop into a ladies room. Droplets of rain
were sliding off her long, straight hair, and her shoes and
panty hose were soaked. When she came to the right door,
she took off her raincoat and slung it over her arm, hoping
she would look less wet. Her navy suit hung limply on her
body—she'd lost twenty pounds during the past few years
and hadn't been able to put it back on. She stood there a
moment, combing her hair with her fingers in a vain effort
to make it look more presentable, then gave up and
knocked.

Marshall's "Come in" sounded a little abrupt to her ears;
she was sure she'd annoyed him by being late. She was about
to apologize when she realized he was in the middle of a
phone call. He waved her into the chair across from his desk

and kept on talking—something about reviewing a colleague's book for a professional journal.

He was more youthful-looking than Jessica had expected, especially given his national reputation, but otherwise he was the picture of an ivory-tower academic. His dark hair was on the long side, not stylishly so, but probably because he hadn't gotten around to going to the barber lately. It grew out every which way, as if the last one to cut it had used an ax instead of a pair of scissors. Jessica noticed the gray at his temples and realized there must be age lines around his eyes as well, but the thick-lensed, black-framed glasses he had on hid so much of his face that it was impossible to tell. Either he'd forgotten to shave that morning or was trying to grow a beard, because the lower half of his face was also hidden—by a layer of dark stubble. He was wearing a nondescript tan cardigan with leather elbow patches over a hideous plaid shirt, and his rumpled black raincoat was hanging on a coat tree behind his desk. Jessica began to feel a little less nervous. Marshall might be brilliant, but there was nothing physically threatening about him.

He hung up the phone, and then, looking distracted, rifled through the papers on his desk until he located Jessica's resumé. "Jessica Lawrence, graduate student at the Brookline Conservatory," he mumbled to himself. "Oh, yes, I remember you now. You're Alex Ulanoff's friend."

Jessica only wished Alex hadn't looked so relieved when she'd told him who had placed the ad. Although Alex had been the one who'd brought the ad to her attention in the first place, he hadn't really wanted her to answer it, which of course had only made her more determined to do so. As fate would have it, Alex had served on a faculty committee with Marshall the previous term and had gotten to know him quite well. He'd insisted on putting in a good word for Jessica, saying she'd be perfect for the job, but what he'd really meant was that Marshall would be the perfect boss—somebody Alex knew, somebody Alex could trust.

It wasn't so much Alex's pull that Jessica minded as his overprotectiveness. The past few years had been like a nightmare at times and Alex's help and support had been a godsend, but he didn't seem to understand that sooner or later she had to learn to stand on her own two feet. As grateful as she was for his help and as much as she cared for him, she also felt he worried too much. He seemed to want to shield her from life's pains and disappointments, but nobody could do that for another human being. Jessica only wished she could make him see that.

If she couldn't, part of the reason was her gentle nature. No matter what black thoughts she might be thinking, she seldom spoke them aloud. Her instinct was to accommodate people, to try to please them. She knew Alex had meant well in speaking to Marshall about her, so she wasn't about to comment on his behavior. She simply smiled and said, "That's right, Dr. Marshall."

He smiled back, but the smile was so distant she had the feeling he barely knew she was there. "I'll tell you what I have in mind and we'll see how you fit in. Fair enough?"

He waited for her nod of agreement, then continued, "I plan to take a look at how Americans use their vacation time. At the moment I'm juggling several different projects at once, so any research I do will have to be very preliminary. I want to travel around, observe how family members interact with each other and other vacationers, and do some interviewing. I need to get a sense of what sorts of issues I should address. If I decide the subject is worth pursuing, I'll outline a plan of study during the fall and winter and get back to the project next summer."

He paused, obviously waiting for Jessica to comment. Since she had very little information to go on, all she could think to say was, "It sounds very interesting, Dr. Marshall."

"Not to most of my colleagues," he replied. "They've nicknamed the project 'The Sociology of Camping,' but I intend it to be much more than that."

In truth, Jessica rather agreed with his colleagues, but Arthur Marshall was a brilliant sociologist. If he felt it was worth his while to study a bunch of tourists, he was probably right. "I'm sure it will be," she said. "I'd consider it an honor to work with you. Exactly what would I be doing?"

"I'll answer that by telling you what happened last spring, when I went down to Florida to do some preliminary interviewing. I've never had a problem getting people to talk, but those tourists would take one look at my tape recorder and clam up. All I got was a lot of platitudes about what a good time they were having. So, I decided to borrow my sister and brother-in-law's camper this summer, find an assistant to pose as my wife, and pass myself off as just another vacationer. I'm hoping that if I tell people my troubles—fictional, of course—they'll open up about their real expectations and disappointments. So, first and foremost, I'll need somebody with a good memory for conversations who can organize what she hears and translate it into concise notes."

He folded his arms across his chest, obviously waiting for Jessica to tell him what a wonderful job she would do, but she couldn't be less than honest. "I'm not sure how good I'd be at that. I can play back a piece of music after I've heard it just once, but conversations aren't the same thing. I have no experience at what you want me to do."

Marshall flipped to the college transcript she'd attached to her resumé. "With grades this good, you shouldn't have a problem."

"Yes. I mean, no, I probably won't. I've never really had to cram—that is, I remember lectures pretty accurately and my notes are only...I don't need to study them very much." She realized she'd been stammering like a nervous schoolgirl, but hadn't been able to help it. Marshall's plans had finally sunk in. Travel around in a camper? Find someone to pose as his wife? Exactly how far did he expect the impersonation to go?

He didn't seem to notice the doubt on her face. "Alex tells me you're easy to get along with. If I'm going to spend over a month in a camper with someone, obviously that's an important consideration. He also says you're quiet, and since I plan to spend my evenings writing the lectures for a new course I'll be teaching next fall, that's a big plus, too."

"But I practice four to six hours a day. I can't be quiet in the evenings if I have to work all day long." The protest was automatic. No matter how much Jessica wanted the job, nothing would be permitted to come between her and her music.

"It won't disturb me." Marshall looked at her resumé again. "The, uh—the flute—is one of my favorite instruments. I'll enjoy having some music in the background. Let me see now. Your address is—ah, here we go. I'll pick you up at ten o'clock Monday morning. It's a large camper, so you can bring along as much clothing as you want."

For a moment Jessica simply sat there, astonished by how easy it had been. Alex must have done an incredible sales job on the man for him to hire her after such a brief interview.

Still, there were questions she needed answered before she could agree to work for him. People tended to underestimate her because she was quiet and slow to assert herself, but when she really cared about something she was quite capable of speaking her mind or digging in her heels. Her grandparents had found that out when they'd tried to ship her off to Europe for college and she'd flatly refused, insisting that her Boston flute teacher was one of the best in the country and she had no intention of leaving him.

Given the intimate nature of her questions, she didn't find them easy to ask, but a few blushes had never killed anyone. "Dr. Marshall, about the sleeping arrangements—"

"You'll be using the sofa in the parlor area. It turns into a bed."

"And you?"

He frowned. "The camper has a separate bedroom, of course. Why do you ask?"

Jessica looked into her lap. "Because you mentioned my posing as your wife—"

"Only when we're conducting interviews. I assumed that would be obvious." Jessica thought he sounded impatient, but when she looked up at him, his bland expression was unreadable. "Are you suggesting that two adults can't work together professionally if one of them happens to be a man and the other a woman?"

When he put it like that, her reservations sounded absurd. "Of course I'm not, but there's a difference between working together for eight hours a day and living together for twenty-four."

"You're wrong, Jessica. There's no difference at all. A man who respects a woman colleague and treats her as an equal during an eight-hour day in an office isn't going to behave any differently if he happens to be traveling with her. I assure you, I don't make a practice of sexually harassing my female assistants."

Jessica felt foolish and inexperienced. Arthur Marshall was an eminent academic, and besides, Alex seemed to trust him completely. She'd obviously offended him by questioning his integrity—the last thing she'd wanted to do.

When she didn't reply, he asked if she had any more questions. She would have liked to know where he planned to go and how much he intended to pay her, but decided both subjects could wait. The job was perfect for her needs, and she didn't want to annoy Marshall any further by bothering him with a lot of unimportant details.

"Not really," she said.

"In that case, I'll see you Monday morning." He stood up and held out his hand. He was taller than Jessica had expected, with broader shoulders and a bigger frame, but not at all tough-looking or even especially masculine. His clothes were worn and baggy, hiding what was probably a flabby, overweight body, and his handshake was brief and limp. Jessica was sure he'd dismissed her from his mind by then and was musing about some intellectual problem. If ever a man was safe, Dr. Arthur Marshall was. He was so wrapped up in his work that a woman assistant could have crept into his bedroom in the camper with seduction on her mind and he never would have noticed she was there.

Griff waited until Jessica had closed the door and then closed his eyes and groaned softly. God in heaven, the girl was a dedicated flute player! Her tooting and squeaking were going to drive him nuts. He made a mental note to get himself a set of earplugs and wondered if there was anything he could do about the rest of her shortcomings.

She couldn't possibly have any talent. Granted, she had done well in school, but he couldn't picture anyone that bedraggled-looking and timorous succeeding at anything in the real world. The only time she'd asserted herself was when she'd started panicking about the sleeping arrangements, although for the life of him Griff couldn't fathom why she would think that any healthy male would have designs on her body.

On the contrary, she was so scrawny he wondered if she were anorexic. Her suit had been at least two sizes too big on her, as though she'd dieted herself halfway out of existence, and her face had been pale and drawn. Her eyes were her best feature, a bright, clear green framed by long, dark lashes, but her black hair had been so lank and stringy that one barely noticed anything else about her face. Even more important, she had no discernible personality—no confidence, no liveliness, no sense of humor. Griff couldn't imagine what a sophisticated, intelligent guy like Alex Ulanoff would see in her.

He straightened the papers on his father's desk, mentally listing what he knew about the man. According to Arthur Marshall, Ulanoff had taught both literature and playwriting courses at Harvard. The two men had served on a faculty committee together but had never socialized. Arthur had remembered Ulanoff asking about Griff's background, but his questions had been so off-the-cuff that Arthur assumed he was simply curious. He'd remarked to Arthur that he'd heard about Griff through his friends in the business community, some of whom had used Griff's services, but the two men hadn't spent more than a few minutes on the topic. The only other thing Arthur had been able to add was that Ulanoff's wit and his tendency to grade generously had made him a favorite with the students.

As far as Griff and Roxy had been able to determine from the calls they'd made, N.E.T.C. had done very well under Ulanoff's stewardship. Between the two of them, they had spoken to most of the local critics as well as various members of Boston's artistic community, and nobody had had anything bad to say. Everyone seemed to consider Ulanoff an excellent fund-raiser and an innovative director. As for his plays, the critics enjoyed his sense of humor but didn't put him in the same class as such playwrights as Sam She-

pard and David Mamet. Several people had mentioned his
father, saying that it must be difficult to live in the shadow
of Nicolai's genius, but having a wealthy and famous father had also had its plus side. One of N.E.T.C.'s more
talkative benefactors had told Roxy that Nicolai had estab-
lished a large trust fund for Alex, enabling him to live much
more comfortably than his salary alone would have permitted.

By the time he and Roxy had finished checking Ulanoff
out, Griff had more or less decided to take the case. He
never cut deals over the phone, so he had arranged to meet
Ulanoff for breakfast the next morning at a Boston restaurant. Ulanoff started things off by talking about Jessica and
her situation, but soon launched into an anecdote about a
famous actor and his outrageous demands. Every now and
then somebody he knew would stop by their table, until a
private meal turned into a party. Obviously Ulanoff wielded
a lot of clout in this town—his friends were prominent
businessmen, politicians, artists and socialites. Since Griff
was as charmed by him as everybody else seemed to be, he
couldn't see a reason not to work for him. He figured he
would even enjoy traveling around New England for a
month in Bill and Sally's camper.

Of course, he had to consider Jessica Lawrence's presence. He was beginning to suspect he would earn every
penny of his twenty-five hundred a week, because when the
girl wasn't driving him crazy with her flute, she would
probably bore him senseless with her torpid personality.
Ulanoff, he decided, must have unusually strong protective
instincts. He'd told Griff that he'd gotten to know Jessica
through her grandparents, who'd been major contributors
to N.E.T.C. during their lifetimes. Judging by the greetings
Ulanoff had received from the women who'd stopped by
their table, he was something of a ladies' man, but Jessica

was apparently the one he really cared about. He saw the girl as sweet and defenseless—a goldfish in a sea of sharks.

She was also an heiress, of course, but Ulanoff didn't seem to need her money. His trust fund more than met his needs. Besides, if it had been money he was after, he would have tried to talk her into voting with her Uncle Charles and selling Lawrence Shoes. Instead he was trying to remove her from a situation that seemed to be causing her a great deal of distress. As far as Griff could tell, he was acting out of love and concern, not from any more selfish motive.

The bottom line was that, starting Monday, he'd be baby-sitting the girl. The polyester monstrosities in his closet were more suited to an office than to a camping trip, so his most immediate need would be to buy some additional clothing. He smiled at the idea, thinking he would have to drop by his parents' place when he was through shopping. His father had agreed to this impersonation with his usual resigned good humor, but the way Griff intended to dress would be the unkindest cut of all. The urbane Arthur Marshall would probably choke with mortification at the sight of all those checks and plaids—assuming he managed to stop laughing long enough.

Chapter Three

Jessica's grandmother had been a hardworking woman, the mainstay of several Boston charities as well as a devoted homemaker, but when her health had started to deteriorate she'd been forced to hire a live-in housekeeper. She'd never been happy about letting somebody else run her home, but Jessica had no such reservations. It wasn't that she was lazy, only that nobody had ever taught her to do anything more than rinse out her panty hose or make herself scrambled eggs. She'd been relieved beyond words when Mrs. MacPherson had agreed to stay on after Ethel and Henry had died.

A motherly widow in her fifties, Mrs. MacPherson shopped and cooked and cleaned, and most of all, fussed. As much as all her hovering and coaxing got on Jessica's nerves at times, she knew she would have been even thinner and more tense if Mrs. MacPherson hadn't kept such a sharp eye on her. Jessica might not eat very much, but Mrs. MacPherson saw to it that she never missed a meal. She never missed a dance class either, even if Mrs. MacPherson had to snatch away her music to make her stop practicing and push her out the door.

Since Mrs. MacPherson watched Jessica so closely, it wasn't surprising that she sometimes noticed things before Jessica did. Looking at the collection of chicken bones on Jessica's plate that night, she remarked, "I haven't seen you eat so well in ages. Getting that job this morning must have meant more to you than you realized."

Jessica stared at the plate in bemusement. She *had* eaten a lot of chicken. "Maybe so," she said, "but I wasn't aware of feeling any different. I was so busy practicing I never even thought about the job."

"Well, whether you thought about it or not, there's nothing like the prospect of a change to get a person's juices flowing again." Mrs. MacPherson cleared away Jessica's plate before Jessica had a chance to do it. "Sit back down and don't you move an inch. I'm going to get you a nice slice of pie and I expect you to eat every bite."

A minute later she was back, carrying an enormous piece of apple pie topped by a scoop of vanilla ice cream, and still talking a blue streak. "It's the best thing in the world for you, getting away from Boston. Alex can be a mite pushy at times, but he was right about that much. Those uncles of yours are a disgrace, fighting like a pair of ferrets before your poor sainted grandfather had even departed this mortal earth. You should call your Aunt Rita in the morning and tell her you're sick. We can go to a movie tomorrow night instead."

Jessica was supposed to go to Ernest and Rita's house in Lexington the following evening to attend their daughter Emily's engagement party. "You know I can't do that," she said. "I'm going to be Emily's maid of honor, and besides, it's not her fault that her father and Uncle Charles are at each other's throats.''

''But they'll start in on you again, the same as they always do. You'll let it upset you and that will be the end of your appetite.''

Jessica was afraid she was right. She was already dreading the party. Every time she had to go to one of these family gatherings, she tossed and turned all night and woke with a throbbing headache. The only thing that ever soothed it was her flute, so she would play until her jaw ached and her arms were ready to drop. Then, at the last possible moment, she would throw on a dress, and, not caring how she looked, drag herself out of the house.

Instead she slept surprisingly soundly and woke with more energy than she'd had in months. Rather than thinking about her music or worrying about whether she'd be able to fend off her uncles, she was full of tasks and plans. First of all, she had to sort through her clothing and decide what to take on her trip. She hadn't bought anything new in ages other than a few T-shirts because she'd kept telling herself she was going to gain weight. Did anything fit her anymore? Was anything in style?

She showered and washed her hair, then slipped into her underwear and started trying things on. She was too thrifty to throw away anything even passably fashionable, but the pile of rejects still mounted up faster than the pile of keepers. She'd always found shopping rather tedious, but suddenly the idea of checking out the summer sales appealed to her. She'd seen the women around town wearing that season's sportswear and loved the way it looked. It was so bright, fresh and bold. She also needed a couple of new dresses; most of what she owned hung on her like sheets.

She pulled on a shift that wasn't quite as loose as her other dresses and picked up her brush. She couldn't even remember the last time she'd gotten a haircut. It hadn't seemed necessary since she wore her hair parted in the center and straight down on each side. She realized it was a long shot given how busy Fridays always were, but decided to call the salon where her grandmother had always gone to see if they could squeeze her in.

That was how Mrs. MacPherson found her—standing in front of her mirror amid piles of clothing with a brush in her hand and a frown on her face. She offered to keep Jessica company while she shopped and Jessica gratefully accepted, but the fact that she was going out with her fifty-eight-year-old housekeeper and not a friend her own age told her something else. She had become terribly isolated over the years.

She saw people in school and at orchestra practice, at her ballet classes and at church, but she never went to restaurants, movies or concerts with them. Her social life had come to consist of evenings spent either with Alex or with one or the other of her uncles and their families. Although she wasn't an extrovert and had never had tons of friends, there had always been a few special ones in the past. Somehow she had let them drift away, until her only contact with them was an occasional phone call or a quick conversation between classes. She decided she would do something about that as soon as she and Marshall got back from wherever it was they were going.

She wound up buying a lot more clothing than she'd planned to; the prices were hard to resist and Mrs. MacPherson kept dragging her from store to store. The new clothes were a little loose on her, but she'd chosen things that way deliberately. She was five foot seven but only a hundred and five pounds, and obviously that was too thin. Years ago, she'd actually had to watch her weight, so she was sure to get up to where she belonged in no time now that she was eating again.

By the time they got to the beauty salon, Jessica was giddy from all the shopping. She told the stylist she wanted to look like Cybill Shepherd and walked out three hours later with a soft, shoulder-length permanent. Her hair was curlier than Cybill's and auburn instead of blond, and the face it framed wasn't nearly as spectacular, but Jessica felt feminine and pretty for the first time in longer than she cared to think about. She found herself looking forward to the party that night—to wearing the green silk dress and seeing everyone's reactions.

At first, everything went just the way she wanted it to. Her cousin Emily told her she looked fantastic. Some friends of Emily's fiancé, Ron, flirted for all they were worth. Her Aunt Rita, who constantly nagged her to eat, saw that she was attacking her food like a starving wildcat and had to keep her mouth shut for once. Her straitlaced cousin Chuck, a law student, announced that he was glad to see the color back in her cheeks, and his younger brother Todd, who was mildly irresponsible, slightly disreputable, and easily the most likable male in the family, teased her about being the next one to get married.

In fact, the first few hours passed so pleasantly that Jessica was lulled into a false sense of security. She was so relaxed and happy she didn't even run for cover when she came out of the upstairs bathroom and saw her Uncle Ernest waiting for her in the hall. Ernest, who was Emily's father, was the uncle who wanted to hang onto Lawrence Shoes. His arguments about tradition and loyalty were so stirring that Jessica invariably felt like Benedict Arnold at the mere thought of selling out.

"Have I told you how nice you look tonight?" he asked.

He had told her three times. "Yes, Uncle Ernest. Thank you."

He peered at her feet, looking at her strappy silver sandals. "Aren't those Fabrinis?"

Antonio Fabrini Footwear was the company Ernest wanted to buy. He'd decided that the high-fashion shoes and boots they manufactured would be the perfect complement to Lawrence's own lines of sports shoes and conservative oxfords and loafers.

Jessica stood there wishing she'd bought something other than Fabrinis to wear with her new dress. She knew what was coming next. "Yes, they are," she said.

Ernest's eyes took on the glow of the dedicated visionary. "*Antonio Fabrini for Chester Lawrence!* Ah, Jessie, I dream about it every night. How proud your grandfather would be! He always wanted to expand into the national market with a line of beautiful Italian shoes. If you believe in an afterlife, as I do, you must know how happy it would make him to own a company like Fabrini."

Fabrinis were manufactured in Massachusetts and not in Italy, but Jessica didn't say so. The few times she'd tried to argue with Uncle Ernest about whether the Fabrini deal was best for all concerned, he'd invoked the name of the company's founder and family patriarch, Chester Calvin Lawrence, who was presumably beaming down from heaven as benignly as Jessica's grandfather at the thought of owning Fabrini Footwear. She gave Ernest a weak smile.

"And think of your father," he continued, warming to his subject even more. "George might have been the youngest son, but he had just as strong a feeling for the family company as I have. He never would have agreed to sell. Never. There's a special pride that comes with making a product for five generations and knowing it's the best there is. There's no substitute for family control, Jessie, no substitute. Big conglomerates don't take the same care with their products that family owners do. They watch the bottom line instead of worrying about quality, beauty and service. It breaks my heart to think of the Lawrence name on shoddy, faddish merchandise. How could I go on if such a thing happened? The betrayal of it—to our history, to my own personal standards! Ah, Jessie, the sheer betrayal of it! I swear to you, I would take a gun to my head and shoot myself before I would allow that conglomerate to get its hands on my company.''

Jessica told herself what she always did when Ernest went on this way—that he didn't mean it, that he was simply being dramatic, that only a gullible child would have taken him seriously. Then she said what she always said. "Uncle Ernest, you know how impossible it is for me to choose—"

"Of course, dear. I realize Charles and Nancy have been good to you, but who gave you a surprise Sweet Sixteen party? Who took you to Europe after college? My God, you and Emily are practically like sisters. I've always considered you a second daughter.''

He gave an exhausted sigh, as if he were bearing the entire weight of the world on his shoulders and couldn't endure it another moment. "But none of that matters. I would never resort to emotional blackmail to get your vote. Tradition is all that matters. People have been wearing our shoes for five generations. They know they can trust us. A Lawrence shoe is a well-made shoe. It's a classic shoe. It's a shoe that fits. Our customers know we'll give them their money back if they're not satisfied. I couldn't have been more than six years old when your grandfather started explaining those things to me. If he were still alive, Jessie, he wouldn't stand for all this talk of selling out—not for a moment. After all, he was the one who negotiated the option to buy Fabrini. Both of us know it's what he wanted, and it's up to all of us to honor his last, sacred wish.''

Jessica stood there for a good ten minutes more, listening to what she had come to think of as The Speech. Ernest was such a rousing orator, it was all she could do not to applaud or salute. She was only rescued when Emily and Ron sat down to open their presents and the sound of everyone oohing and aahing began to drift upstairs.

She looked around for Alex when she got down to the living room, but he hadn't arrived yet. He was practically a member of the family and was always asked to these sorts of get-togethers, but he'd had a last-minute invitation to have dinner with a corporate president who was thinking of donating a large sum of money to N.E.T.C. He couldn't afford to turn the opportunity down, but he'd promised Jessica he would get to the party as soon as he could. For all her talk of independence, Alex was the one she turned to when the pressures got too intense. She might wish he were less protective, but she also recognized that nobody was better at running interference for her than he was.

Ernest had waited to catch her in private but Charles wasn't so discreet. As soon as Emily and Ron had finished opening their gifts, he walked up to Jessica, put his arm around her shoulders, and announced, ''I got some new figures from my accountant yesterday. I hope you'll do me the courtesy of looking at them.''

Jessica did her best to put him off. ''Even if I did, Uncle Charles, it wouldn't make any difference. I've tried to explain—''

''You were talking to Ernest for at least twenty minutes,'' Charles interrupted. ''Don't you think I merit the same consideration?''

Jessica's stomach started to churn. Damn it, where was Alex? How long could his dinner drag on?

She noticed Emily watching them, saw the strained look on her face, and sighed. Emily had a stake in this, too, because Ron was an executive with Lawrence Shoes. Emily didn't say anything, but then, she didn't have to. Her tight mouth and narrowed eyes said it for her. She was furious at Charles for starting in on Jessica during her engagement party. Her own father had done the same thing, of course, but that was different. Ernest and Emily were on the same side.

Jessica gave her an apologetic look and followed Charles into the den. She was resigned to hearing his version of The Speech, which she had come to think of as The Lecture. Unlike Ernest, who relied on emotional arguments about pride, tradition and loyalty, Charles took an economics professor's approach. The spreadsheets he shoved under her nose made very little sense to her, but she obediently followed along as he pointed to number after number and explained what each of them meant.

Her eyes were bleary by the time he finally finished. "In terms of the return we'll get, we're never going to do better than this," he insisted. "The way this deal is structured, you'll never have to worry about money again in your life, Jessica. My parents might have left you a generous amount, but it won't last forever. This will take care of your future."

As Jessica knew full well, it was only due to Charles that she could afford to live in her grandparents' Beacon Hill home, employ Mrs. MacPherson and remain in school. Originally her grandparents' estate had been divided into three equal portions, just as the Lawrence Shoe stock had been. Charles had persuaded them that, as a classical musician, Jessica would never be able to earn the same kind of income as he and Ernest. Therefore it was only reasonable to make some additional provision for her. As a result they had changed their will, leaving her their house and a modest trust fund as well as the Lawrence Shoe stock and a third of their other assets.

She owed Charles a second debt as well, one that was far more important to her than financial security. Her grandparents had been practical Yankee merchants with little patience for anything so frivolous as a career as a classical musician. They had wanted Jessica to forget about the flute and learn the family business. The only reason they hadn't started brainwashing her at the age of six as they had their three sons was that she hadn't come to live with them until she was eight. Of all her relatives, only Charles and Nancy had taken her side. They were the ones who had interviewed and hired a first-rate music teacher for Jessica when she was a young teenager and ready for expert instruction; they were the ones who had paid for her music camp in Michigan every summer. Jessica's grandparents had eventually come around, turning into her staunchest supporters, but that wasn't until she had finished her third year of college and had made a brilliant debut as a soloist with her school orchestra.

Still, however much Charles had supported her, he wasn't going to sway her by appealing to her supposed need for security. "I'm not worried about my future," she said. "If I can't get the orchestra job I want, I can always earn a teaching credential and give music lessons on the side. You of all people should understand that a fancy house and a full-time housekeeper don't matter to me that much. Only my art does. We've talked about this before."

"I know that, Jessie, but your attitude doesn't make economic sense." As usual, Charles was becoming impatient with her. A hard look came into his eyes, making Jessica straighten and draw back a little. He rustled the spreadsheets in extreme agitation. "This offer is a gold mine. It isn't as though they want to throw Ernest out on his backside. They've already committed themselves to keeping him on as president until he retires. A Lawrence will still be running the company and we'll all be set for life. Isn't that good enough for you?''

Jessica flushed nervously, intimidated by the passion in his voice. "But what about after Uncle Ernest retires?'' she asked.

"Emily's not interested in running the company and neither are you or my own two boys. That leaves Ron, who's not even a Lawrence. Face facts, Jessica. The days of family control are over.''

He had a point, except that Ron was just as devoted to Lawrence Shoes as Uncle Ernest was. Ron and Emily were fighting the sale because they didn't trust big conglomerates, either. Like Ernest, Ron was more interested in quality than in profits, and he was afraid his priorities would eventually get him dismissed.

It wasn't easy, but Jessica somehow forced herself not to back down. "Emily and Ron's children will have Lawrence blood and so will mine, if I ever marry. So will your own grandchildren. If the issue is whether or not a Lawrence will ever be in charge again, the chances are that one will.''

Charles couldn't prove otherwise, so he shifted his grounds of argument to the personal, replacing his sarcasm and impatience with a kind of angry pleading. He wasn't interested in shoes—Jessica knew that. Like her, he was an artist. Hadn't he supported her at every turn because of how much he'd empathized with her? Where the devil did she think she'd be if it hadn't been for him and Nancy? What he wanted most in the world was to quit his job at Lawrence and devote himself to his painting, but he could only afford to do that if the sale to the conglomerate went through. Unlike Jessica, he was too old to suffer for his art. Besides, he had a wife to support and two sons who were still in school.

Jessica sympathized with him, but she also sympathized with Ernest and Ron. By the time she finally got away, her queasiness had turned into a full-blown bellyache. Fortunately, Alex had arrived by then, and he could tell by the look on her face that she'd had a tough time of it. He got her away from her relatives as soon as he possibly could.

They wound up out on the terrace, talking quietly. "I felt so good when I woke up this morning," she said. "I was excited about working for Marshall and relieved to be going away. I went shopping, I had my hair done—I felt wonderful. Then Ernest trapped me in the hallway, practically threatening to kill himself if I don't vote his way, and Charles..." She shuddered. "Charles frightens me at times. He's so determined to sell, it's almost irrational. And then there's Emily. She doesn't even have to say anything, just look at me. Oh, Alex, she's like a sister to me. How can I vote against her and Ron?"

Alex put his arms around her and drew her close. Jessica felt a little of the tension drain away as she rested her head against his shoulder. "None of them is being fair to you, sweetheart. The wisest course of action is to stay out of it." He backed up a couple of steps and smiled down at her. "I like your new hairdo, and the dress, too. You *must* have been feeling better, to take so much trouble with how you look."

Jessica felt herself redden. "Because I'm usually such a mess, you mean."

"Oh, God, that didn't come out right. I meant that I realize how difficult things have been and I'm glad you're finally feeling better." He tucked her arm in his and led her toward the side of the house. "I don't think we need to go back inside to say good-night. They've upset you enough for one evening."

As they walked around to their cars, he suggested they go out for dinner the following evening—a farewell meal. He was going to miss her every moment she was gone and wanted her to have a special night to remember him by. As if to prove it, he took her in his arms and gave her a lingering kiss on the mouth instead of his usual peck on the cheek.

Jessica stood motionless, too surprised to respond. She understood that Alex thought of her as a woman and not a child, but he'd been careful not to make demands, careful not to push her. He'd known she had too many pressures in her life to cope with a romantic involvement. His patience had apparently run out now, but Jessica didn't know whether that was good or bad.

As she stepped into another of her new dresses the following evening, she realized how unusual their dinner out was. She and Alex went to concerts or the theater at times, but never to parties or fancy restaurants. He knew she found it an effort to dress up. Tonight, though, she actually enjoyed it. She was so relieved to be leaving Boston Monday morning that not even her uncles' squabbling could upset her for long.

She and Alex talked about the usual subjects during dinner—art, music, the theater. The service was elegant and unhurried, the food delicious, and Jessica took full advantage of both. When Alex made a teasing comment about how much she was eating, she smiled and said she would only be able to indulge herself that way for another couple of weeks.

"I was kind of chubby as a child," she explained. "I'd managed to slim down by the time you met me, but when Grandmother got sick—"

"You stopped eating. I know. You can't imagine how relieved I am that you've finally gotten your appetite back." He reached into his pocket and took out a small package. "Jessica, I hadn't planned to bring this up before you left, but you'll be gone for so long, and Marshall is a very—well, never mind that. Just open it."

If Jessica hadn't had almost as much wine as she'd had food, she might have been embarrassed or apprehensive. As it happened, she was merely surprised. The package could only contain one thing—a diamond ring. Alex was very dear to her, but she hadn't expected him to propose. As much as he seemed to care for her, he was also a confirmed bachelor. She'd never imagined his feelings ran so deep that he'd be willing to make a permanent commitment.

She took out the ring and held it up to the light. "It's lovely, Alex, but I don't think we're ready for this kind of decision. You've been a wonderful friend all these months and I'm grateful for all you've done, but we've never gotten to know each other as equals. We need more time to find out if we're right for each other."

"I love you, Jessica. Surely you must realize that." He slipped the ring onto her finger. "I'll be much happier if I know you're wearing this while you're gone. I suppose you think it's a primitive reaction, but I can't seem to help it. You looked so beautiful last night."

It took Jessica a minute to figure out what he was talking about, and once she did, she couldn't help giggling. "My lord, Alex, you can't possibly be worried about Dr. Marshall! The idea is ridiculous."

"Why is it so ridiculous?" he demanded. "You'll be traveling with him for the next month, living in his camper and sleeping only a few yards from his bed. Naturally I'm worried—and jealous."

"Of Arthur Marshall?" Jessica couldn't keep the astonishment out of her voice. "Good grief, Alex, he's almost old enough to be my father!"

Alex frowned. "He's younger than I am, Jessica."

"You're kidding!" Jessica took a sip of wine, thought about it for a moment, and gave a dismissive wave of her hand. "Well, even if he is, it's not the same thing at all. For one thing, you look so much younger than he does. And for another, you act so much younger. Besides, Marshall is the original absentminded professor. Well, maybe not absentminded, exactly, but in his own private world. Wrapped up in his research. I'm not surprised he isn't married. He's probably never noticed there are two different sexes."

She caught a flicker of bewilderment on Alex's face, but it passed so quickly she decided she must have misinterpreted it. "Marshall is a very brilliant man," he said. "Surely you find that attractive."

"I suppose so, but his brain isn't what would kiss me. His mouth is." She screwed up her face in distaste. "What a disagreeable thought. That horrible haircut and awful stubble... And besides, his body was so—so sexless, so soft. I wouldn't even want him to touch me."

Alex's bewilderment returned in full force, but this time he couldn't hide it. After a long couple of seconds, he murmured, "I've never heard you talk that way before."

"You've never gotten me tipsy before. I'm not an angel, Alex. I do notice whether a man is attractive or not." She took off the ring and put it back in its box. "If you proposed to me because you were worried about Dr. Marshall, don't be. The man is—he's practically a eunuch. Nothing's going to happen between the two of us."

Alex stared at the ring, apparently lost in thought. Finally he took it out of the box again and held it out. "Wear it for me, sweetheart. You've had a rough time of it over the past couple of years and I can understand why you wouldn't be sure of your feelings for me, but I don't have the slightest doubt about mine for you. I love you very much and I want to marry you. We don't have to set a wedding date yet. I want you to be as sure of how you feel as I am. But in the meantime..." He caught hold of her hand and drew it closer. "Please. Humor me and wear it."

Jessica cared for Alex very much and couldn't picture herself with anybody else. Not only was he attractive, he had everything she'd ever wanted in a husband—intelligence, culture, kindness and charm. His request wasn't all that unreasonable, so long as he understood that she wasn't agreeing to a formal engagement.

"There's nobody else," she said. "You know that. I don't think we need symbols to show that we mean something to each other, but if having me wear the ring would make you feel better—"

He cut her off before she had a chance to finish. "It would. I need some kind of commitment from you. That's what engagements are all about—or should be, anyway. They're a time to test your feelings, to make sure a marriage would work. You were right before. We need time to get to know each other as equals. In the meantime, I need some sign that you're serious—even if you don't, Jessica."

Jessica allowed him to slip the ring back on her finger. While she couldn't promise to marry him, she could certainly keep an open mind about it. That was all he was really asking, and given all that he'd done for her, she was more than willing to agree.

Chapter Four

Dr. Arthur Marshall had struck Jessica as such a fog-brained intellectual that she half expected him to forget he'd even hired her. At a minimum, she was sure he'd be late picking her up, but he appeared on her street almost exactly at ten, driving a thirty-foot Fleetwood motor home with a motorcycle strapped to its back. How somebody so preoccupied as Dr. Marshall was going to maneuver a vehicle the size of a dinosaur in Boston traffic was anybody's guess, but that was why God had given the world seat belts. As for the idea of hopping on the motorcycle with him, Jessica was only sorry she hadn't gotten around to drafting a will.

She walked over to greet him as he braked to a stop, telling herself she should probably reintroduce herself. Given her new hairstyle, the five pounds she'd gained and the fact that her clothing no longer fit like a tent, he might not place her right away. "Good morning, Dr. Marshall," she said. "I'm Jessica Lawrence."

He gave her a blank stare out the open window. His hair, she noticed, was as spiky as ever and his face was just as stubbly. "Who else would you be?" he asked.

"I thought you might not recognize me. I do look a little different."

He squinted at her through his thick glasses, as if he were wondering if he could conceivably have missed something important. "Your hair—did you do something to it?"

Jessica decided there was a lot to be said for such stunning obliviousness. At least Marshall didn't judge women the way most men did, by making snap judgments on the basis of their personal appearance. "I got it cut," she said, sure it would be a waste of time to tell him what else she'd done. "My things are just inside, packed up in cartons. Should I start bringing them out?"

He opened the door and hopped out of the camper, saying he would give her a hand. Given his total lack of concern with his own looks and clothing, it was little wonder he didn't pay the least attention to anybody else's. He had on baggy red-and-yellow checked pants, a blue plaid polyester shirt, and an ancient-looking acrylic cardigan similar to the one he'd worn on Friday, except that it was an indiscriminate maroon tweed instead of a solid tan. Jessica had come across her share of ill-dressed professors in her time—sartorial disasters were something of a tradition in academia—but none of them had held a candle to Arthur Marshall. She decided he must be color-blind.

Mrs. MacPherson's eyes widened incredulously when Jessica brought him into the house, but she managed to keep a straight face as they shook hands. Between the three of them, they carried Jessica's things to the camper in a single trip, bringing them in through the door in the center of the right-hand side. Marshall immediately sat down behind the

wheel, prompting Jessica to leave the cartons on the floor
rather than begin to unpack them.

She'd never been in a motor home before and was im-
pressed by how comfortable and well-equipped it was. The
front section contained a dinette and sofa in addition to the
driver's and passenger seats; the kitchen and bathroom took
up the middle third; and there was a bedroom furnished
with a double bed in back. Overhead cabinets lined the walls
on the sides and in back, providing plenty of storage space,
and a sliding wooden door between the bedroom and bath
area and lighter folding door between the bath and galley
ensured privacy.

Jessica would have liked to take more than a quick look
around, but Marshall seemed impatient to leave. After
hugging Mrs. MacPherson good-bye and promising to
write, Jessica closed the center door and settled into the seat
on Marshall's right. He hadn't said a single word since his
hello to Mrs. MacPherson and didn't say anything now.

He rolled up the window a little and pulled away from the
curb. Between the crowded city streets and the recklessness
of the local drivers, Jessica found herself gripping the edges
of her seat. She was sure they were going to hit something,
either a traffic sign, a parking meter, or another vehicle, but
eventually she began to relax. Marshall might look like he
wouldn't know a baseball from a tennis racket, but he had
the alertness and quick reflexes of an expert athlete. He
handled the camper as if he'd been driving it all his life.

She didn't expect him to talk while they were still in city
traffic, but his silence continued even after they'd picked up
the Massachusetts Turnpike. To the extent Jessica had
thought about her job at all, she'd seen it mostly in terms of
escape. She hadn't asked herself what sort of relationship
she and Arthur Marshall would have, hadn't worried about
how they would get along. Maybe she'd pictured herself lis-

tening in on interviews and writing up notes, and maybe she'd mused about seeing her name in the acknowledgments section of the book he planned to write, but she'd never stopped to consider whether a month in his company could possibly be anything but an improvement over a month of being pressured by her Uncles Ernest and Charles. Marshall was a little eccentric, of course, but as far as she could tell, the job would be close to a paid vacation.

Now she wasn't so sure. She had nothing against quiet people—she was quiet herself—but Marshall seemed to be downright antisocial. Never mind asking how she was or chatting about the weather; he hadn't spared her so much as a passing glance. In fact, he hadn't even told her where they were going. She studied him out of the corner of her eye, wondering what was going on in that brilliant mind of his. The intimacy of the camper made her uncomfortably aware of how much younger she was than he; how much less experienced; how much less knowledgeable. He looked so unapproachable that she was almost afraid to speak, but one of them had to break the ice and obviously it wasn't going to be him.

"I was wondering about our itinerary," she said.

There was no reaction. She figured he hadn't heard her, so she raised her voice a bit and tried again. "Have you worked out our itinerary in advance or are we going to play it by ear?"

"I have reservations in Lake George." He glanced in the left-hand mirror and pulled out to pass. "We'll stay there three or four nights."

"And then?"

"We'll see."

"So you haven't made any plans beyond that?"

"Obviously not, Jessica." His tone said that only an idiot would have had to ask.

Intimidated, Jessica leaned back in her seat and stared out the front window. Maybe Marshall didn't like to talk while he was driving. It probably took a lot of concentration to control a vehicle this big.

Another few minutes went by. Increasingly restless, Jessica stared at the radio in silent longing. Finally, screwing up her courage again, she asked Marshall if they could listen to some music while they drove.

In lieu of an answer, he switched on the radio and jumped from one station to another until he found one that was playing a current rock song. As a musician, Jessica appreciated talented, creative composers no matter what field they happened to write for, but she preferred the classics to the Top 40. The ballad on the radio was overly sentimental and predictable, the musical equivalent of a Saturday morning cartoon. Obviously Marshall had no taste in music, but anything was better than dead silence. She turned her attention back to the window and tried to take an interest in the scenery.

They passed the cutoffs to Worchester and then Sturbridge. Jessica had gotten up at six that morning and her stomach was starting to rumble, but she didn't want to annoy Marshall by suggesting they should stop for lunch. Lake George was four to five hours away, but perhaps he preferred to drive straight through and get it over with. The prospect of spending the next month with the man got more and more daunting with each passing mile, but at least it didn't affect her appetite. She would have killed for a chocolate bar, let alone a decent meal.

He exited the highway near Springfield, turning north toward the city of Holyoke. Jessica would have settled for a hamburger or a slice of pizza by then, but Marshall drove into town instead of stopping at a fast-food place. He never asked Jessica if she was hungry or where she wanted to eat;

he simply parked the camper and got out, walking until he found a restaurant he liked, expecting her to follow along. She was beginning to understand that the usual social graces meant nothing to him.

They were halfway through lunch before he said anything that didn't pertain to his order, and even then, his comments were directed to the waitress. He wanted to know where he could find a jewelry store that sold plain gold wedding rings. The waitress's eyes darted to the diamond ring on Jessica's left hand as she answered Marshall's question. The diamond was large enough to attract attention, not that Marshall had noticed it.

Jessica waited for him to explain what he wanted with a wedding ring, but he didn't seem to feel it was necessary. Maybe it wasn't, given the fact that she was going to pose as his wife. A little irritated by his silence, she tried to think of a way to confirm his intentions without asking what he would consider to be another stupid question.

In the end she tried to make a joke out of it. "I guess I'm in for an interesting month—being engaged to one man and married to another. Tell me, Dr. Marshall, do you plan to wear a ring, too?"

"No." He took a sip of coffee, obviously finding nothing amusing in her comments. "Who are you engaged to? Alex Ulanoff?"

"Sort of. It's a complicated situation." Jessica looked for a hint of interest, for some sign that Marshall wanted her to continue. Although he didn't say anything, he did keep looking at her, which was probably as much encouragement as she was going to get. "I couldn't promise Alex I would marry him, but I told him I would think it over. It seemed to be important to him—to have me wear the ring—so I agreed."

"Then the ring doesn't mean anything," he stated.

"Of course it does." Jessica wondered if he'd even been listening. "It means that I care for Alex very much—that I want to make a commitment to him."

"So what's stopping you?"

"Nothing, except—we don't know each other very well. I need more time."

The question that came next was so logical, it was embarrassing. Marshall wanted to know when they'd met. Jessica realized that three years would seem like a long time to be sitting on the fence, so she tried to explain why she hadn't been able to make up her mind.

"The problem is that we've never had a normal relationship. I was raised by my grandparents. They were in poor health when Alex and I met—it was three years ago—and they had to be my first priority. Both of them are gone now. Alex couldn't have been more supportive and sweet, but we've never had a chance to find out how we would get along in more normal circumstances."

Marshall raised an eyebrow at her and asked dryly, "Are you saying he's magnificent in a crisis but falls apart when things are going well?"

Jessica was aware that he was mocking her, but never would have replied in kind. It took a lot more than mild sarcasm to provoke her. "I really don't know, Dr. Marshall. That's why I haven't agreed to marry him."

"I see," he said, but Jessica doubted it. He looked bored with the whole subject. She didn't attempt to start the conversation again and neither did he.

By the time they left the restaurant she'd decided he had absolutely no sense of humor. Someone like Alex would have made a game out of buying the ring, playfully acting out the role of her devoted fiancé, but Marshall was almost grim about it. He asked to see a tray of plain gold bands, instructed Jessica to pick one out, and paid for it with a traveler's check. The minute they were out of the shop he handed her the box and ordered her to put the ring on. She was sorely tempted to ask whether he planned to recycle it if he got married for real, but knew he would only give her one of his unnerving stares and proceed to ignore her. She kept her mouth shut.

Since her attempts to talk to him hadn't been too successful, she was relieved to get back to the camper. The silences were less awkward when they were driving. Unfortunately, no sooner had he put the key in the ignition than he dropped his hand and settled back in his seat. Obviously he had no intention of going anywhere just yet.

"I could use a break," he said. "Would you mind driving for a while?"

There was no way Jessica was going to get behind the wheel of this monster. "I'm not used to something so big. I wouldn't feel comfortable—"

"There's nothing very complicated about it. It's got power brakes and steering—even cruise control." He started to get up, saw that she wasn't budging, and frowned. "It's only a camper, Jessica, not a Stealth bomber."

It was also more than thirty feet long, and the only way to tell what was beside you or behind you was by using the two side mirrors. Jessica didn't trust anything unless she could see it directly with her own two eyes. She repeated that she wouldn't feel comfortable driving and apologized, then sat there enduring the full force of Marshall's displeasure. He didn't keep pressing her, just turned back to the steering wheel, and, shaking his head at how hopeless she was, started the engine.

They arrived at Lake George late that afternoon. Jessica was tired from the trip and looked forward to unpacking and unwinding, but, as usual, Marshall didn't consult her about her preferences. Instead of going directly to their campground, he pulled up in front of a grocery store, took out his wallet and handed her five crisp twenty-dollar bills. "I need to make some phone calls. I'll pick you up when you're done shopping. Wait for me right here."

"Shopping for what?" Jessica asked. "I mean, I haven't checked the cupboards—"

"For everything. Not pots and pans or dishes—the camper is fully equipped—but everything else. There isn't even a bar of soap in the bathroom."

"Are there any particular foods—"

"Buy whatever you want."

Marshall had a way of making Jessica feel so totally inept that she couldn't bring herself to admit that her shopping experience consisted of running out to the store every now and then for a last-minute item. Her grandmother or Mrs. MacPherson had always done the shopping. Even when she'd gone along, she'd never paid much attention to what cuts of meat they'd selected or how many pounds of a fruit or vegetable they'd bought. She had no idea which sizes to buy. How much detergent did you need for a month's worth of laundry? How much dish liquid for a month's worth of dishes?

She was standing in the store, telling herself that a college graduate should be able to figure such things out, when two elderly women passed by, laughing and chatting as if they had all the time in the world. Inspiration suddenly struck, and along with it an almost comical sense of relief. Jessica hurried after them and tapped one of them on the shoulder. Then, contriving to look even more lost than she felt, she explained that she was a newlywed on a camping honeymoon whose husband had given her a hundred dollars to stock up on food and supplies. Unfortunately she was new at housekeeping and didn't know what to get. Could they possibly help her?

They could and they did. Not only did they escort her through the entire store, helping her decide what to buy; they assured her in no uncertain terms that no bridegroom worth the name would leave a young bride on her own this way. They even insisted on waiting out front with her shopping cart while she ran to a nearby liquor store for some wine. She had just returned when Marshall pulled up in the camper.

The elder of the two women, who was by far the more outspoken, let him know what she thought of him the moment he opened his door. "I don't know what this world is coming to. In my day, a man didn't expect a girl to work on her honeymoon. He coddled her and tried to please her. If you want your marriage to succeed, young man, the least you can do is pitch in and help. This sweet little girl is your wife, not your slave."

Marshall squared his shoulders, looking down his nose at the woman as if she were a singularly unpleasant variety of insect. "I beg your pardon, madam?"

She wasn't the least bit intimidated. "It's your wife's pardon you should be begging, young man, not mine." She turned to Jessica. "Go ahead inside, dear. Let *him* carry in the bags."

Jessica looked at the ground, biting the inside of her lip to keep from laughing. She would have loved to be able to speak to Marshall that way, but he was her boss and she didn't want him to fire her. Besides, he was a high-and-mighty professor who'd written God knows how many books while she was only a lowly student. Since *she* couldn't tell him off, she was delighted that somebody else had done it.

Marshall was scowling as he got out of the camper, but meekly took hold of the shopping cart and pushed it around to the side door. Jessica would have followed, but her protector took her by the arm and wagged a scolding finger under her nose. "Oh, no, you don't! I've been married for over fifty years to a very strong-willed gentleman, and let me tell you, the only way to handle a man like that is to stand up to him. Go inside and sit down. Don't let him browbeat you."

Strong-willed or not, the woman's poor husband had probably never stood a chance. Jessica smiled and thanked her, then hopped into the camper and slid across to her seat. A few seconds later Marshall opened the side door and started carrying in groceries. Jessica didn't dare get up to help. Her two protectors were watching her every move through the side window.

She heard a series of soft thuds as Marshall tossed the bags onto the floor, then a forceful slam of the side door. She was expecting another dose of disapproval, but instead he smiled sardonically as he took his seat, looked out the window, and gave the two women a cheery little wave.

"Delightful pair," he muttered as he pulled away. "What did you tell them? That I kept you chained to the stove?"

"They think we're on our honeymoon," Jessica replied. "They were helping me find things."

"It figures." He sounded more disgruntled than ever. "You seem to inspire protectiveness in people."

He was probably thinking of Alex as well as the two women. "In some people, yes," Jessica agreed. She would have liked to add that he was a clear exception, but held her tongue and consoled herself with the thought that he wasn't as humorless as she'd supposed. His good-bye to the two women had actually been kind of funny.

Also on the plus side, he knew where he wanted to go and exactly how to get there. Jessica was surprised by that; he'd struck her as the type who muddled his way through life. Then again, one couldn't design complicated research projects and write prize-winning books without being well organized, so his appalling personal appearance and general air of distraction had to be anomalous little quirks.

The campground he'd chosen was only about five miles from Lake George Village and looked more like a five-star hotel than the rustic hideaway Jessica had pictured. There was a sizable group of buildings near the entrance, presumably containing shops and recreational facilities, and every conceivable outdoor amenity was located in the park beyond—a swimming pool, tennis courts, a baseball field, basketball courts, a children's playground, even a pond to fish in. At a minimum, the athletic facilities would keep Marshall out of her hair. It wasn't so much that he'd be using them himself, but that he'd be chasing down the people who *were*, in order to interview them.

The sites themselves were in a thick pine wood and contained full hookups. While Marshall went outside to connect everything, Jessica set to work putting things away. The main wardrobe in the bathroom area was empty, and more than big enough to hold her clothing and toiletries. She tucked her tape recorder and tapes as well as her flute, music and music stand into the cabinet over the sofa, and then started on the eight bags of groceries. The bin above the galley held pots and dishes, but the floor-to-ceiling pantry next to the stove was empty, as was the refrigerator. It only took a few minutes to store everything away.

Marshall, meanwhile, had evidently disappeared. Jessica went outside and looked around, but there was no sign of him. Then, curious about what a distinguished professor of sociology would bring along on a camping trip, she went into his bedroom and started checking through his cabinets. The clothing wasn't a surprise—all of it was equally tasteless—but the golf clubs and tennis racket were. She couldn't picture him doing anything physical.

Even more unexpectedly, the built-in nightstand beside the double bed had keyholes in addition to the usual recessed latches. Jessica tried the drawer on top and then the cabinet door below it, but both were locked. Even a rather forceful shake and rattle didn't get the drawer open. She would have like to believe the nightstand contained something more exciting than research materials Marshall didn't want disturbed, but it probably didn't. The man was nothing if not prosaic.

Yawning, she stood up and turned to leave. Then she nearly jumped out of her skin, because Marshall was standing in the doorway, his hand tucked lazily into the right pocket of his trousers. He didn't look especially annoyed, only amused. Even so, Jessica couldn't help reddening. She knew she'd had no business searching his room.

He took a set of keys out of his pocket and held it up. "Do you want to take a more thorough inventory, Miss Lawrence?"

Jessica wanted something much more complicated—to sink through the floor and disappear. "I'm sorry. I just wondered—I was looking around the camper, at all the little nooks and crannies. There's so much room…" Her voice trailed off. What she'd been doing was trying to force open a drawer he'd deliberately locked, and both of them knew it.

"Ah, yes, the miracles of modern design. It's amazing how much storage space they can fit into a vehicle this size." He took a few steps forward, giving her room to pass. "If you would excuse me?"

Jessica couldn't wait to get out of the bedroom. The day had been filled with a series of small humiliations, and the only good thing she could find to say about it was that it was almost over with.

She kept her eyes straight ahead as she crossed in front of Marshall, but was stopped in her tracks by a soft "Jessica?"

She looked back over her shoulder. "Yes, Dr. Marshall?"

"I'm going to lie down for a while. Since I've been driving on and off since nine-thirty this morning while you've been sitting and doing nothing, do you think it would be unreasonable of me to ask you to make dinner? According to your friends from the store, that is."

It wasn't unreasonable at all, except that Jessica didn't know how to cook. "The stove—"

"Works the way any stove does. Just turn it on."

Jessica pressed her lips together. He thought she was either lazy or stupid, she wasn't sure which, but anybody with half a brain could fry a steak and toss a salad. "In that case, I'll call you when it's ready."

Marshall nodded and pulled the sliding wooden door closed. Jessica thanked the gods for small favors. At least she wouldn't have to cope with him standing and watching while she fumbled her way through the next half hour.

On the other side of the door, Griff sighed heavily and dropped onto the bed. If today was a fair sample, the next month was going to seem like a year. He regretted ever taking Ulanoff's phone call. In fact, if Vicki hadn't been such a good secretary, he might have fired her for talking him into it.

Jessica Lawrence had to be the most timid, wishy-washy female he'd ever had the misfortune to meet. True, he'd done his best to keep her intimidated and off balance, but it had been ridiculously easy. A little silence, a curt answer here and there, and she'd been totally unnerved. Anyone else would have demanded more details about where he planned to go, but not Jessica. He could have been hauling her off to California for all she knew. And then there was that business about Ulanoff's ring—a new adornment that Griff had noticed right away. How could she know the guy for three solid years and not be able to make up her mind whether or not to marry him? Either she loved him or she didn't. She'd called it a complicated situation, but as far as Griff could see, it was simple.

The girl was scared of her own shadow, not to mention scared of driving a vehicle that both his sixteen-year-old niece and his fifty-seven-year-old mother had driven with no problem. Sure, they'd been a little nervous at first, but they'd learned. Anybody with a driver's license... The thought brought him up short. Good Lord, was it possible she didn't know how to drive but was afraid to admit it? Anything seemed possible by now. After all, he was talking about somebody who'd had to recruit help just to find her way around a grocery store.

Griff gave another long-suffering sigh and stared at the ceiling. His complaints were seventy-five percent rationalizations and he knew it. There was nothing all that wrong with Jessica Lawrence—it wasn't a sin to be shy and quiet. What *really* got under his skin was that he'd pulled up in front of her house expecting to see a frog and found a princess waiting there instead. Jessica was too damn scrawny for his particular taste, but there was nothing wrong with the rest of her. Her hair wasn't black and stringy—it was a warm chestnut in color, full, wavy and sexy as all get-out. Her face wasn't pale and drawn—she had skin like blushing porcelain, a soft, provocative mouth, and vulnerable green eyes that made him feel like a heel every time he let loose with one of his verbal darts. And the body—the body might have needed a good ten to fifteen pounds and the clothes might have been a little loose, but the curves were exactly where they belonged and the muscle tone was perfect. The last time he'd seen such beautiful breasts, the head upstairs had contained compressed air. Whatever else Jessica was, she wasn't stupid. He knew that from her college transcript.

Even worse, she wasn't the ambivalent little mouse he wanted to believe she was. Ulanoff was determined to marry her, but she hadn't allowed him to railroad her into it—not yet, at least. A mouse would have been mortified by that scene in front of the grocery store, but Jessica had enjoyed every minute of it. He could still see her trying not to laugh at the way her battle-ax of a protector had chewed him out. Worst of all, she'd had the spunk to search his room. Griff had no idea what he would have done if she'd called his bluff and taken the keys he'd held out. He didn't want to have to explain away his gun or his father's lecture notes— the notes he was supposedly going to spend the next month writing. Unfortunately he had the sinking feeling that if he left Jessica to her own devices, she was only going to get bolder. Next time he might not be able to intimidate her into backing off.

He was walking a tightrope here. As much as he regretted taking this case, he'd taken it and he meant to see it through. Professional pride was involved.

He had to keep Jessica in line, keep her from asking too many questions or suspecting he wasn't what he pretended to be. In other words, he had to keep her thoroughly cowed. He couldn't afford to be too nasty about it, though, or she would take the next bus back to Boston.

He closed his eyes, pictured her soft, full mouth and firm breasts, and muttered a heartfelt curse. She was just another job, just another case. Even more to the point, Alex

Ulanoff was a man of no small influence in the Boston area and he meant to marry her. Griff couldn't afford to forget things like that.

Chapter Five

Jessica was standing in front of the stove, giving herself a pep talk. How many times had she sat in the kitchen, keeping her grandmother or Mrs. MacPherson company while they fixed dinner? Hundreds, probably. And hadn't she helped with the shredding and peeling and slicing? Of course she had. She wasn't a total novice when it came to cooking. There was no reason she couldn't make a complete meal—potatoes along with the steak and salad—and have it turn out perfect. *Then* let Marshall give her one of those looks that said she had the brains and initiative of a canned pea!

The logistics of the operation couldn't be all that complicated. If she peeled the potatoes, put them in to boil and then started the steaks, she should have plenty of time to put together a salad while everything was cooking. Telling herself that organization was the key to success, she took out the proper pots and utensils and got down to work.

She wasn't the fastest peeler in the world, so the water was boiling by the time she was finished with the potatoes. They

were on the large side, so she cut them in half before toss-
ing them in the pot. The frying pan she planned to cook the
filets in had a nonstick finish, but she put in some butter just
to be on the safe side. Then, when the butter was sizzling,
she added the meat.

Her first compromise with the goal of perfection came
when she was slicing tomatoes for the salad and realized that
something was burning. She jerked her head to the left, saw
smoke and spitting grease rising from the fry pan, and,
without stopping to think, pulled it off the flame. Then she
cursed and stuck her hand under cold running water; the
metal handle had been red-hot.

The only apparent damage was to her temper, which
started to simmer, and to the steaks, which were charred
black on one side. Forcing herself to calm down, she set the
steaks on a plate and washed out the pan. Then she started
all over again with the steaks on the uncooked side, using a
lower flame this time.

It wasn't low enough, though, because the same thing almost happened all over again. Fortunately, the second side
of the steaks had only gotten crisp, not burnt, but the cen-
ters had stayed totally raw. Jessica lowered the flame still
more and went back to work on the salad. Every now and
then she made a cut in one of the steaks to make sure she
wasn't overcooking them.

The salad wound up filling the largest bowl in the cup-
board, but Jessica told herself they could eat the leftovers
tomorrow—and probably Wednesday, too. With the steaks
just about cooked, she drained the potatoes and returned
them to the pot to mash. They fought back valiantly, resisting her efforts for all they were worth. She was trying to
glare them into submission when Arthur Marshall strolled
out of the bedroom.

She added salt, butter and milk to the pot and kept on mashing. Marshall sat down at the table to wait, watching her in his usual preoccupied way. Jessica was perspiring by then and well aware that the meal would be something less than a triumph. Abandoning the recalcitrant potatoes for the moment, she set the table and brought over the salad and a bottle of dressing.

Marshall sniffed the smoke-filled air, then suggested blandly, "It might be a good idea to open a window."

"I'll do that," Jessica said, tight-lipped. Why hadn't *he* opened the stupid window? She was approaching the end of her tether as she angrily twisted the window's handle. It had been a long day, and besides, nobody had ever told her she'd be expected to drive or shop or cook. One critical word out of Marshall and she was going to take his spaced-out head off.

She mashed the potatoes as best she could, put the steaks on a platter, and carried everything to the table. Just so Marshall would understand her mood, she set the food down with more force than was strictly necessary.

Marshall being Marshall, the gesture went straight over his head. Jessica was just about to sit down when he asked, "Did you buy any beer?"

His question was the last straw. The same Jessica who was never rude or sarcastic gave him a murderous look and snapped, "If you'd told me to buy beer, I would have bought beer!"

He nodded to himself. "I take it the answer is no."

It was all Jessica could do not to kick him. "You take it right, Dr. Marshall, but even if I had—"

"Griff," he interrupted.

Startled into momentary silence, Jessica tried to figure out what he'd said. It had sounded sort of like a dog growling. "What was that?" she asked.

"You've got to stop calling me Dr. Marshall." He gave her a lazy smile. "My family calls me Griff—it's short for my middle name, Griffin. I don't like being called Arthur, at least not by the people who are closest to me." The smile got a little wider. "People like my wife...*Mrs. Marshall.* Now what were you saying about the beer?"

Jessica had been about to tell him that even if she *had* bought beer, he could darn well get it himself, but she was so nonplussed by his behavior she forgot she was even angry. Had Arthur—no, *Griff* Marshall—actually been trying to charm her into a better mood? It wasn't possible.

"I'll pick some up tomorrow," she said. "There's wine, and also milk and soda—"

"Wine would be fine."

"White or red?" Jessica had bought both.

He smiled again. "You mean I have a choice?"

The teasing note was back in his voice—not just teasing, Jessica realized in astonishment, but husky and sort of sexy. Utterly befuddled, she took a closer look at him. Despite his soft body, dreadful haircut and thick glasses, he wasn't all that bad looking. If he'd bothered to give himself a decent shave, he might even have been halfway attractive.

She gave him a sheepish look. "I may not be the greatest cook in the world, but I do know good wine. If you want red, there's a Mondavi cabernet and also a French burgundy."

"Now I know why there wasn't any change," he drawled, referring to the money he'd given her to shop with. "Make it the burgundy."

"A hundred dollars doesn't go that far these days," Jessica informed him pertly. "I paid for the wine myself—my treat, Dr.—uh, Griff." She fetched the bottle from the pantry, uncorked it quickly and expertly, and brought it to the table.

She assumed the atmosphere would be more congenial from that point on, but it wasn't. Not only did Griff clam up, he expressed his opinion of the food with a silent eloquence that was far more scathing than mere words would have been.

His first taste of the mashed potatoes had him grimacing and grabbing for some wine, and Jessica soon found out why. The potatoes were lumpy and undercooked, and worst of all, too salty. He cut the charred meat from his steak with all the precision of a surgeon, inspected what was left, and sighed. Jessica had been trying to cook the steaks medium rare, but she'd forgotten to take them off the stove while she was struggling with the potatoes and they'd turned out medium well. The way he ate his meat was an indignity all its own—he chewed it doggedly and methodically, as if consuming it was the act of a total martyr. The only thing besides the wine that seemed to please him was the salad—he had three helpings of it.

Jessica was directing all sorts of black thoughts at his head by the end of dinner, but he took the fuel out of her fire by offering to clean up. She immediately started to feel guilty. Whatever else he'd done, he hadn't complained aloud, and the meal *had* been rather dreadful. The men in Jessica's family never set foot in the kitchen, so how could she allow Griff to do so? It was on the tip of her tongue to refuse.

Then she remembered all the articles she'd read about two-career couples, modern marriages and how women were always getting the short end of the stick when it came to the housework. Just because her uncles and cousins were unregenerate male chauvinists, that didn't mean Griff should be. If they were going to live together and work together, he could do his share of the chores.

There was no question that she needed some time alone. Griff was bewilderingly unpredictable—preoccupied and silent one moment, sardonic or even biting the next, and finally, when she least expected it, downright charming. She'd found it a strain to be in his company, and even more of one to be by herself and try to shop and cook when she barely knew how to do either. A walk around the campground with no Griff Marshall to hover over her and no chores to do sounded like heaven.

He was already clearing away the dishes, so she told him she'd be back in half an hour, grabbed her jacket out of the wardrobe, and left. She'd been walking for about a minute when she came across a group of people standing under a sign that read Tram Stop. They explained that shuttle buses circled the park all day long, ferrying people between their campsites and the many recreational facilities. Jessica decided to take a ride around.

The driver kept up a steady patter of jokes and information, eliciting both laughter and groans from his passengers. Everyone seemed to be having such a marvelous time that Jessica began to think she and Griff had come to the wrong place. These people weren't worth interviewing and analyzing; there was nothing dramatic or mysterious about their lives.

She got off the tram near the entrance into the park and headed for the complex she'd noticed when they'd first arrived. She quickly realized that there was so much to do, you could spend your whole vacation here and not get bored. A band was playing in a large recreation hall and people were dancing. Smaller rooms in the building next door contained Ping-Pong tables, pool tables and a video games arcade. There was a grocery store and a variety store, a snack bar, a lounge with a fireplace, and even a movie theater. Jessica bought herself a couple of magazines in the variety store and then returned to the rec hall lobby where there was a large bulletin board listing current and upcoming activities.

She'd read over the notices and was about to leave when a woman not much older than she was walked over and introduced herself. "I'm the recreation director, Karen Davis. I don't recognize you. Did you just get in?"

Jessica was amazed that she could remember whether or not they'd met. There were hundreds of campsites in this park. "We arrived this afternoon. I'm Jessica Lawrence—uh, Marshall. Jessica Marshall." She smiled weakly. "I'm not used to the name yet. We haven't been married very long."

"You're on your honeymoon, then?"

Karen was probably wondering why a new bride would be on her own. "Yes, but my husband's a teacher and he's got a new course to get written while we're gone. I came down to look around. It's amazing—all the facilities you've got here."

"Well, it's my job to see that everybody uses them." Karen pointed to a notice on the bulletin board. "You don't happen to have any talent, do you? We put these shows on every Wednesday and I'm always trying to recruit people to appear in them. You don't have to be all that good, just a good sport and a bit of a ham."

Jessica loved to perform, but was afraid classical music might bore people, especially children. "I play the flute, but—"

"The flute? But that's perfect! You did bring it along, I hope."

Jessica nodded, wondering if Karen was this enthusiastic about all her discoveries. It turned out she was a singer and actress who had taken the rec director job for the summer. She always performed in the shows, had the music for "Send in the Clowns" in her office, and thought a flute would sound wonderful with her singing. Would Jessica appear with her?

They went back to her office for the music and then sat down in the snack bar to discuss it. The arrangement was scored for piano, so Jessica would have to pick out a melody line to play on her flute. They agreed it should be part accompaniment and part counterpoint—that the flute and the vocalist should perform a sort of duet together. Jessica promised Karen she would get back to her the following evening, bringing down her flute for a run-through.

It was lovely outside, brisk but not too cold, and Jessica wasn't in any hurry to get back to the camper. She studied a diagram of the park that was posted outside the recreation complex and then set out on foot, stopping for a while to watch a tennis match and then joining in a game of pickup volleyball. By the time she returned to the camper, over an hour and a half had gone by.

Griff stalked out of his bedroom the moment she opened the door. "Do you have any idea what time it is? I was just about to take my cycle and look for you. In case you didn't notice, it's dark out there."

He reminded Jessica of Alex, fretting about her safety as if she were an irresponsible child. Maybe that was why her reaction was so immediate and so strong. "It's just past nine, I was down at the rec center, and it's still light enough to see where you're going."

"You said half an hour." He walked over to the camper door and locked it. "I was worried. It's a big place, and I thought you might have gotten lost or even hurt. I didn't think you were the type to disappear."

Normally, Jessica wasn't, but maybe that was because the people in her life had always kept such a close eye on her. She liked the idea of being able to come and go as she pleased, of not having to account to anyone for her actions. Still, Griff's concern had obviously been genuine and she could see that he was tired and out-of-sorts. She didn't want to argue with him, so her only alternative was to coax him into being more reasonable.

"I have a good sense of direction and there are signs everywhere you look," she said. "Believe me, nobody tried to assault me, but even if they had, I'm sure one of the security people would have protected my honor. You can't go anywhere around this place without running into one of their patrols."

Griff didn't seem either placated or amused, so Jessica tried a slightly different approach. "I'll tell you what, Griff. If you don't worry about me, I won't worry about you. Is it a deal?"

He stared at her for a long couple of seconds, mumbled a grudging agreement, and marched back to his room. Jessica shook her head, wondering what he was so grumpy about. She wouldn't understand him if she spent the next year with him.

It was late and she was tired, but she hadn't practiced her flute that day and didn't want to skip it. She didn't want to disturb Griff, either, so she set up her music stand as far from his room as she could. Then she took out her scale and exercise books. If she was only going to practice for an hour or two, her technique had to come first.

She ran through some scales to warm up, then played an exercise she'd had the devil's own time mastering. It would have sounded all right to a casual listener, but Jessica knew the notes had been too breathy and the fingering too clumsy. She took it a section at a time after that, playing each passage over and over until she was satisfied with the results.

She'd been practicing for almost an hour when Griff came stomping out of his room, looking more tired and grumpy than ever. "Are you trying to drive me crazy?" he demanded. "Punishing me for worrying about you? Trying to get yourself fired? Because that damn song you're playing is the most annoying, boring piece of music I've ever heard, and if I have to listen to any more of it I'm going to take that blasted flute and turn it into a pretzel."

Jessica was more amused than it was safe to admit. Griff was almost human when he got flustered and cranky. "It's an exercise, not a song," she said mildly, "but if it annoys you, I'll play something else."

"The hell you will. Put away the flute and go to bed, Jessica."

He was treading on dangerous territory now. "You agreed I could practice—"

"I didn't realize my sanity would be at stake." Before Jessica realized what he meant to do, he'd darted forward and grabbed the flute out of her hands. "You can have this back in the morning."

Jessica's eyes narrowed. Nobody messed with her flute and got away with it. She couldn't have been any angrier if he'd manhandled one of her arms. "Flutes are like people," she said in a deceptively quiet way. "They have their individual quirks and characteristics. The one you're holding has a lyrical, mellow quality so beautiful it could break your heart. It took me years to find. It also happens to have cost me a fortune." She named the exact figure and then held out her hand. "Give it to me, Dr. Marshall—very carefully."

She never thought she would see the day when Griff Marshall blushed, but he did—a dramatic shade of red. "I'm sorry," he mumbled. "I didn't realize—I have a horrible headache and I didn't stop to think." He handed her the flute, avoiding her eyes. "I suppose you can really play this thing."

"I'm not James Galway or Jean-Pierre Rampal, but I do okay." Now that Jessica had her flute back, she began to soften. Griff seemed to be in a lot of pain. "About your headache—have you taken anything for it?"

"Nothing helped."

Despite her self-effacing reference to the giants in her field, Jessica knew she was unusually talented. She wanted Griff to know it, too. "Somebody once said that music had charms to soothe a savage breast. I could play—"

"It was Congreve, and this particular savage breast needs peace and quiet, not music. I'm exhausted, but I can't fall asleep as long as you're playing."

"That's because I was playing the wrong piece of music," Jessica said. "Trust me."

He only gave in because it was obvious that was the quickest way to shut her up. By the time Jessica had found the tape recording she wanted and brought it into his room, he was lying in bed with an arm flung across his eyes. She put the tape in her recorder, wound it forward to the proper spot, and clicked it on. Lilting, enchanting music filled the room.

"Piano?" Griff mumbled.

"The accompaniment to the concerto I'm going to play you part of. I recorded it myself, to play along with it. It's more fun that way."

He gave a low grunt. "You're a good pianist."

"I'm an even better flutist." Jessica smiled to herself, waiting for the first movement to end. Then she began to play the second movement of James Galway's flute adaptation of Mozart's Concerto in G for Clarinet and Orchestra. Even the gods themselves couldn't have written anything more achingly lovely or richly melodic, but then, there were those who said that Mozart had been touched by the divine.

The music was so gentle and soothing she was sure it would put Griff to sleep, but he pulled away his hand after she'd finished playing and had clicked off the tape. "Don't stop," he said groggily. "That was nice. Play the last movement for me."

Their eyes met and held. Jessica had never realized what a warm shade of brown his were. He looked so much younger without his glasses, so much more vulnerable and approachable. She felt a trembling warmth in the pit of her stomach but ignored it and clicked the tape back on. A minute later Griff moaned softly and rolled onto his side. He was fast asleep by the time she finished playing.

Chapter Six

Jessica rolled onto her side, gave a sniff, and wondered why Mrs. MacPherson was cooking bacon in her bedroom. It took her a moment to remember that she was sleeping in a camper and that the person cooking the bacon had to be her boss, Griff Marshall. Still logy with sleep, she sat up and tugged at the strap of her nightgown. Griff was standing by the stove, watching her in his usual preoccupied way. Given the hours professors usually kept, she'd expected to be showered and dressed before he even woke up, but here she was, still in bed, wearing the equivalent of a satin slip. Griff could have been watching the neighborhood mutt for all the interest he seemed to have, but Jessica grabbed her robe and hastily pulled it on. Her modesty was wasted, because he'd already turned back to his cooking.

"I'm playing golf today," he said. "You can do whatever you want. I'll leave you a set of keys to the camper."

And good morning to you, too, Jessica thought. Had this man had no mother? Had nobody ever taught him the basics of civilized behavior?

She resisted the urge to wince as she got out of bed. Today's outfit was even more hideous than yesterday's—green and yellow pants in a bold check, a golf shirt with purple and white vertical stripes, and a yellow-brown sweater with overtones of bilious green. The sweater reminded Jessica of the way a jar of Gulden's mustard would have looked if it had eaten something that disagreed with it.

She started toward the bathroom. Griff had taken some eggs out of the refrigerator and was cracking them into a bowl. "I'm making omelets," he said. "They'll be ready in five minutes." He glanced over his shoulder at her as she passed by. "You could use a few extra pounds. You're too scrawny."

Jessica wanted to smile sweetly and offer to take a couple of his, but it was a brand-new day and her tolerance was in long supply. Besides, the man was cooking breakfast for her. His domestic talents went a long way toward compensating for his assassination of the social niceties.

She only took the time to wash up and brush her hair, but she still looked tidier than he did. It wasn't that he was dirty—on the contrary, his clothes were spotless and his hair was freshly shampooed. Sitting across the table from him, she could smell the clean scent of his soap. But every garment he owned seemed to be baggy and ill-fitting, his hair invariably looked as if it had been blown dry by a mad scientist, and he always had the same three-day stubble. Either he thought it looked sexy or he had the world's worst razor, Jessica couldn't imagine which.

She was about to compliment him on his cooking when he pointed to the spice rack by the stove. "I noticed a bottle of MSG over there. Did you use it on the steaks?"

She nodded. "One of the women from the grocery store said it would bring out the natural flavor of the beef—not that there was much flavor left by the time I got through burning it."

"MSG gives me headaches," he said, oblivious to her attempt at humor. "Don't use it again."

Jessica would have been annoyed by his curtness if she hadn't felt so guilty. She'd read that MSG caused headaches in a lot of people, so why hadn't she checked with Griff before she'd dumped the stuff all over his steak? She'd caused him an agonizing couple of hours, not to mention a probable case of indigestion.

She reddened, nodded again and concentrated on finishing her breakfast. Griff didn't say another word, just rose from the table, picked up his golf clubs and left her to clean up. Even though it was her turn, she was irked that he hadn't discussed it with her. He was either arrogant or hopelessly boorish, she couldn't decide which.

Either way, a day out of his company looked better all the time. Jessica spent the morning practicing her flute and then caught the shuttle to the rec center and ate lunch in the snack bar. On her way out of the building she ran into Karen Davis, who asked if she'd had a chance to work on their duet. Jessica promised she would get to it later that afternoon and arranged to meet Karen at seven-thirty for a rehearsal.

In addition to running trams around the grounds, the campground provided hourly transportation into Lake George Village. One of their vans was sitting about twenty feet away, waiting until it was one o'clock to leave, and Jessica made a spur-of-the-moment decision to hop on board. It was a beautiful day, perfect for window-shopping in town.

She was walking past a drugstore when a display of picture postcards caught her eye. Nobody except Alex and Mrs.

MacPherson knew she was gone, but people would notice eventually. Jessica didn't want anyone to know where she was, but there was no harm in sending out some postcards. She could mail them the day they left Lake George.

She paid for the cards and was about to leave the store when she noticed a mouth-watering illustration on the cover of one of the monthly food magazines. She flipped to the recipe—*Daube de boeuf à l'ail*—and decided it was something she could manage. Since it wasn't in her nature to hold grudges, she'd pretty much forgotten that Griff had a rare talent for driving her up the wall. What she remembered was that dinner had been dismal while breakfast had been perfect, and that she'd nearly poisoned him with MSG. She wanted to prove she could cook a decent meal, if not to him, then to herself. She bought the magazine and continued over to the market, buying the ingredients she needed for the stew. She also picked up some beer, telling herself that if Griff didn't like the brand it was his own darn fault for not being more specific.

She expected him to be home by the time she got back but was just as glad when he wasn't. She had to get the stew into the oven as soon as possible and didn't relish the idea of him hovering over her, watching. In her fantasies, he would appear in a couple of hours, sniff air that was redolent of beef, tomato and wine, and swoon in sheer ecstasy.

The name of the dish translated into English as "casserole of beef with garlic," but it contained onions and various vegetables as well. The recipe called for an entire head of garlic, which seemed like a lot but apparently wasn't, because the flavors mingled and mellowed during the long, slow cooking process. Forty minutes later Jessica set the casserole in the oven and congratulated herself on her efficiency. All she had to do was add the vegetables and warm the French bread, and dinner would be ready. Griff would surely be back by six—no round of golf took more than eight hours to play.

With half the afternoon still in front of her, she settled down to work on her duet with Karen. Like most musical people, she could hear harmonies in her head, so it was easy to sketch out a flute part. Then, just for fun, she recorded the vocal and played the two together. After making a dozen or so changes, she put the piece aside and started practicing a Vivaldi sonata.

The stew was simmering nicely by then, giving off a strong aroma of garlic. Jessica thought it smelled wonderful—it reminded her of her Italian grandmother's kitchen. She only wished she'd saved some of the garlic for garlic bread.

At five-thirty, she skimmed the fat off the stew and added the vegetables, and twenty minutes later she put the bread in to warm. Six o'clock came and went, then six-fifteen. Jessica turned down the oven to "warm" and continued to practice. By six-thirty she was too agitated to concentrate on her music. Where was Griff? Didn't the man have the least consideration for anybody else's schedule? Didn't he care that some people might prefer to eat at a sensible hour or that they might have plans for later in the evening?

By seven she was quietly furious. Of course he didn't care. She'd known that since yesterday, so how could she have permitted herself to forget it? She sat on the sofa and glared at the door, ready to scald him with disapproval the moment he crossed the threshold.

Naturally, he never noticed. He strolled in with his golf clubs, and, barely looking at her, gave an exaggerated sniff. Then, grinning widely, he asked, "Was somebody attacked by a vampire last night?"

Jessica was in no mood for stale jokes. She made a show of looking at her watch and announced, "It's past seven."

"Is it?" He set his golf clubs on the floor and went to the sink to wash his hands. "I played two rounds. Is dinner ready yet?"

Jessica could barely contain herself. What did he think she was, his personal slave? He wasn't even grateful she'd cooked dinner. He'd simply expected it! Without a word, she marched to the oven and took out the casserole and bread. Griff was already at the table, sitting there like some medieval potentate. She shoved the food under his nose, stalked over to the refrigerator, and returned with the left-over salad and some beer.

Griff opened the beer and took a sip. "Is something wrong?" he asked, looking totally bewildered.

Jessica didn't even know where to begin. The man was so dense she had to hit him over the head just to get his attention, so how did she explain that he had the worst manners since Conan the Barbarian? She silently counted to five— very slowly—and then said evenly, "You left at seven-thirty. I thought you'd be back this afternoon. I had no idea where you were and no way to track you down. You might have called the campground office and asked them to give me a message about when to expect you."

He frowned at her. "We have an agreement, Jessica. You don't worry about me and I don't worry about you. We come and go as we please, remember?"

He cut himself a slice of the bread, which was so hard from over an hour in the oven that it crumbled on contact. Fortunately, the butter had been sitting on the table the same length of time and was soft enough to spread without destroying what little of the bread remained. Griff had no sooner taken a bite than he grimaced and set the bread back on the table. It had to be dry as dust by now.

Jessica watched in silent frustration. He was right about their agreement, so how could she complain? He spooned out some stew and she did the same. She wasn't surprised that the piece of potato he stabbed with his fork should disintegrate into mush. After all, she'd cooked it three times too long. On the other hand, at least the meat wasn't tough—stringy, yes, but not tough.

As for the flavor, it was a good thing Jessica liked garlic. Griff apparently didn't share her enthusiasm, because he ploughed through the meal with the same martyrlike determination as the night before. Jessica's temper started to simmer when he cut another slice of bread, this time from the middle of the loaf, and sighed heavily when he realized it was almost as hard as the ends. Even worse, he washed down bite after bite of food with long swallows of beer. When he finally finished eating, he took out a roll of breath mints and popped one into his mouth. Jessica somehow held her tongue, but then he made a fatal mistake. He spoke, and what he said was, "I think we'll eat out tomorrow night."

She set down her fork, goaded beyond all endurance. "You didn't say anything about cooking when you hired me, Dr. Marshall, but I've done the best I can. I timed everything for six o'clock. If you'd shown up by then, the bread would have been soft and the vegetables would have been firm. I'm sorry you don't like garlic, but I followed the recipe exactly. I even made a special trip to the store to get the ingredients I needed. And I made a point of buying you some beer—with my own money, by the way. It might be nice if you paid me back."

She took a deep breath, trying to get her emotions under control. Confrontations had a way of making her eyes well up with angry tears. "I'm supposed to be down at the rec center right now, going over a song for the talent show tomorrow night, but instead I've been sitting here for the past twenty minutes getting silently insulted. If you're not satisfied with me, why don't you just say so? I can be on my way back to Boston on Thursday."

In spite of her show of bravado, returning to Boston was the last thing Jessica wanted to do. As much as Griff could upset her, he was better than her two uncles. Still, she was tired of feeling inadequate, tired of trying and failing, and tired of being either ignored or condescended to. Every now and then she'd seen a flash of humanity in the man and she refused to believe he couldn't be more civil if he really put his mind to it. After all, he was as stuck as she was. He needed a research assistant, and it was a little late in the game to hire somebody different.

She'd hoped for an apology, but that was obviously the dream of a fool. Ignoring most of what she'd said, he repeated, "Talent show? What do you mean?"

Jessica no longer had the self-control to explain. "It's not important," she mumbled, and stood up.

He caught her by the wrist to keep her from leaving. "You're supposed to be at some kind of rehearsal?"

When she didn't answer, he prompted, "You're playing the flute?"

Jessica tugged at her wrist. "Dr. Marshall—"

"Is that what's going to happen every time you get mad at me? You're going to call me 'Dr. Marshall' in that cool little voice?" He loosened his grip on her wrist and smiled crookedly. "You play the flute like an angel, and nobody expects angels to be gourmet cooks. I'm sorry I gave you a bad time about dinner. You probably should have dumped it over my head. And I'm sorry I made you late for your rehearsal. Grab whatever you need and I'll run you down to the rec center on my cycle."

There it was again—that easy, confident smile and warm, sexy voice. Befuddled, Jessica mumbled her agreement and went to get her flute. How could you stay angry with a man who apologized so contritely and flattered your musician's ego so appealingly?

She was so wrapped up in trying to figure him out that she completely forgot that his motorcycle had once evoked thoughts of wills and life insurance. He gently pushed a helmet onto her head before they went outside, making her feel feminine and protected. The lithe male grace with which he swung his leg over the seat of his cycle hardly gibed with her image of preoccupied, disheveled professors. Bewildered, she got on behind him and held him tightly around the waist. It wasn't until she got off that she realized how different he'd felt from Alex or her uncles. Underneath those baggy trousers, Griff Marshall had the solid gut of a prize fighter. Even more astonishing, she'd enjoyed every moment of the ride—enjoyed the scent and touch of him and enjoyed the warmth of his body. She didn't know which puzzled her more—the contradictions in Griff's character or her mercurial reactions to him.

Jessica was learning to be realistic when it came to Griff, so she wasn't surprised when he reverted to form the next morning and curtly informed her that he'd decided to take another couple of days off and planned to play some more golf. She simply smiled at him as she'd smile at an ill-mannered child and enunciated every syllable of the words "good morning." Then she stood with her arms folded across her chest until he got the message and replied in kind. They didn't talk during breakfast—he made pancakes this time—but he promised to be back by five and told her not to bother cooking. If he didn't return in time to make dinner, he said, they would go out. Jessica felt a devilish urge to tease him and didn't bother resisting it, answering that of course she would see to dinner since she planned to hang around the campground all day. She thought he looked a little green as he walked out the door.

It was such a beautiful day that she took her flute outside and practiced under the pine trees. Every now and then somebody would stop and listen, but Jessica didn't allow herself to be drawn into lengthy conversations. If she chattered, she wouldn't get enough practice in.

After lunch, she went into town. Although she hadn't been entirely serious about making dinner, cooking was turning into a nemesis to be conquered. The problem, she decided, was that she'd tried to be too fancy. She needed to fix something foolproof—something like lasagna, for example. Between a good basic cookbook and her favorite bottled spaghetti sauce, what could go wrong? She'd assemble the lasagna in advance, only putting it in the oven once Griff actually got home.

A few hours later she sprinkled the last of the grated cheese over the top of the lasagna and put it into the fridge. She knew she should practice some more but was too restless to sit still. For all that she complained about how exhausting her daily dance classes were, she missed the physical exercise.

She changed into a swimsuit and took the tram down to the pool. A lane had been roped off for lap swimmers, but nobody was using it. Jessica dove in, started a slow but steady freestyle, and let her thoughts wander aimlessly. When she finally climbed out, she was amazed to find that a whole hour had gone by. Pleasantly tired now, she settled into a deck chair and began to read.

Clouds gradually blew in, giving the air a distinct chill. Although reluctant to leave, Jessica finally pulled on her cover-up and headed toward the nearest tram stop. Then, remembering the row of phone booths inside the rec hall lobby, she decided to call Alex and Mrs. MacPherson first.

She'd promised to keep in touch but hadn't sent so much as a postcard yet. The least she could do was tell them where she was.

She was in the middle of dialing Alex's office when the voice in the next booth made her stop in mid-number. Griff was speaking, asking for somebody named Roxy. Jessica wasn't normally one to eavesdrop, but Griff had begun to intrigue her so much that any new tidbit of information was irresistible. She quietly hung up the phone and pressed her ear to the wall.

Griff had gotten into the habit of checking with Roxy every afternoon, something she insisted wasn't necessary but which the workaholic in him couldn't give up. She claimed nothing exciting ever happened but he doubted she was telling the truth. After all, he kept claiming the same thing.

He hadn't admitted that Jessica was beginning to attract him, or that he'd made a stupid mistake like letting her see him without his glasses the night she'd played the flute for him. The damn things had been tucked away in the bin over his bed and he'd been half-asleep by then, but that was no excuse. Even worse, his initial strategy just wasn't working. She didn't retreat into her shell or scurry out of his way when he tried to intimidate her. She simply got more and more frustrated, until some unpredictable thing pushed her over the edge and her temper exploded in his face.

He could tell himself from now till next month that the only reason he turned on the charm on such occasions was to placate her, but the truth was more complicated. He hated upsetting her—it made him feel like a two-bit bully. He didn't want to crush her spirit, either—not when he enjoyed the way she scolded and teased him. God help him, but he was even starting to feel protective toward her. He no longer had to ask what Ulanoff saw in her.

In her own quiet way, she was a fighter. She refused to let him browbeat her. Too much more of her cooking and he'd be as skinny as she was, but she refused to admit defeat in that department, either. And skinny or not, she filled out a satin nightgown in a sensational way. Griff hadn't figured out how something less revealing than a bathing suit could do such dramatic things to his blood pressure; he only knew it was safer not to appear in the kitchen until she'd gotten into her robe each morning. He'd found to his chagrin that it was safer not to give her motorcycle rides, either. He could still feel the warmth of her breasts against his back, still remember the way she'd clung to him. She was spunky but vulnerable, stubborn but eager to please, maddeningly appealing and far too much of a challenge. And there was no way he was going to admit that to Roxy Pascal. He'd been a little too arrogant about how easy it would be to handle Jessica.

"So how's it going?" he began. "Are things falling apart without me?"

Roxy simply laughed. "Don't you wish! How's Lois Lane, Superman?"

"She keeps trying to poison me. Last night it was a stew with enough garlic in it to kill the entire population of Transylvania. I don't think she knows how to cook."

"Poor Griff!" Roxy didn't sound very sympathetic. She thought Griff was appallingly chauvinistic when it came to his expectations of women and their domestic skills. "So what did you do today? Play golf?"

"Yeah. Sooner or later I'll have to do some interviewing, but I'm not looking forward to it. The weather's been great."

"And Jessica's not suspicious?"

"Not as far as I can tell," Griff said. "If you want the truth, I think she's glad to get rid of me every day. I can't blame her for that. I've given her a hard time."

"Which is probably why she wants to poison you," Roxy pointed out. "Simple revenge. I'll bet she's really another Julia Child."

"James Galway, maybe, but not Julia Child," Griff said with a laugh. "If there's nothing we need to discuss—"

"There is, actually. I had a call a couple of hours ago from Emily Lawrence. She's Jessica's cousin—Ernest's daughter. He's the uncle who refuses to sell. Emily told me her cousin had disappeared—that nobody knows where she is. She asked me if I could find her."

Griff frowned. "Why you? Did you ask her how she got your name?"

"As far as I can tell, it's one of those crazy coincidences. She went to school with my sister, Francine. You know Francie—one word from me about any of my cases and she embroiders a whole story around it. I guess Emily remembered that Francie had a sister who was a private detective and called for my number. I didn't know whether to choke or laugh when she asked me to find Jessica. Just think, Griff—we could milk this one for thousands. I could be traveling around on vacation, charging her for my time and expenses."

Griff teasingly reminded her that honesty was the best policy, prompting her to laugh and admit she was kidding. But despite the bantering back and forth, he didn't like the way this sounded. Coincidences made him uncomfortable.

"Tell her you're too busy," he said, suddenly all business. "You can mention I'm out of town."

"Will do," Roxy agreed. "Is there anything else?"

Griff absently tapped a golf club. "I don't know. That phone call—I just don't like it. I can't get past the feeling that something may be going on here besides a crazy coincidence. Maybe we should find out a little more about Ulanoff. About Jessica's relatives, too. Do you have time to do that?''

Roxy told him in a sultry tone that she always had time to do what he wanted and hung up. Griff was lost in thought for a while. He was supposed to be working for Ulanoff, keeping Jessica safe so his client could marry her when she got back, but somewhere along the line he'd started protecting Jessica for Jessica's sake, guarding her from Ulanoff, her relatives and anybody else who might want to harm her. He'd never been especially good at keeping his emotions out of his cases, but he'd gotten in faster and deeper on this one than ever before. Shaking his head at the folly of it, he dropped in another couple of coins and dialed his sister's house. She'd had some problems with the camper and he wanted to assure her that everything on board was working perfectly. Everything, he thought ruefully, except his common sense.

Chapter Seven

Dinner, for once, was a triumph. Jessica knew the lasagna must be good when Griff put the first forkful into his mouth, swallowed back his astonishment along with the food and tried not to grin. He'd been his usual distant self till then, but their eyes met over the table and something crackled back and forth. His only comment was "This is very good," but Jessica could sense the barriers momentarily dropping.

She no longer doubted he'd erected those barriers on purpose—that they weren't a usual part of his nature. She'd heard him admit as much during the phone call she'd overheard. Fortunately, he didn't suspect a thing—she'd slipped away afterward, beating him back to the trailer by a good twenty minutes.

If anything, he puzzled her more than ever now. Judging by his tone on the phone, Roxy was a woman—a girlfriend or perhaps a colleague. Jessica had sat there trying not to laugh during his disgruntled remarks about her cooking, but the rest of it . . . *Why* was he giving her a hard time? What was that bit about a phone call? And why had he asked Roxy to find out more about Alex and her relatives?

Obviously Alex had told Griff a good deal about her situation, but something else seemed to be going on here. If Griff hadn't been who he was—a well-known professor and a personal friend of Alex's—she might have been a little unsettled. As it was, she was merely curious. She regarded the unanswered questions as pieces of a fascinating puzzle.

She was tempted to mention the phone call just for the pleasure of one-upping Griff but decided it would be a tactical mistake. Once he got his guard up, she would never find out what he was up to. Only one possibility had even come to mind.

Once, in her second year of college, Jessica had volunteered for a psychology experiment supposedly about human memory and learned much later that it had actually been designed to test the differences in how men and women reacted to anxiety. The experimenters had lied to the volunteers because it was the only way to get unbiased results. Maybe this was the same sort of thing. Maybe Griff was studying something completely different from recreation and Jessica was part of the experiment. She couldn't imagine why a sociologist would be conducting research that was normally in the province of psychologists, but with professors you never knew.

Still, as she watched Griff from across the table, it seemed ridiculously fanciful to think he was anything but what he claimed. He looked so entirely harmless—a middle-aged professor in his own private world who dressed abominably and treated people with casual disregard because he was prominent enough and brilliant enough to get away with it.

Jessica was used to his long silences by now and didn't attempt to start a conversation. He was eating everything she'd cooked with enthusiasm for once, and it was enough.

She wasn't even annoyed about getting stuck with the dishes after dinner. She simply smiled knowingly at the way he dragged himself out of his chair and drawled, "A little too much golf?"

He took a couple of steps forward and winced. "I think I might have pulled a muscle. It's my own damn fault for running around like a teenager." He continued on to his room, moving like a stiff old man.

Given how sore he was, Jessica was surprised when he opened his door a short time later and announced he was accompanying her to the talent show. She suggested it might be wiser to spend the evening in bed, but he answered that the show was too important to pass up. "An authentic slice of Americana," he called it, and added that he planned to interview some of the participants once it was over.

Karen Davis was standing by the entrance to the rec hall when they arrived, handing out photocopied programs. "We're one of the last acts," she said to Jessica, and held out her hand to Griff. "You must be Mr. Marshall. Your wife and I are going to be a smash, but I guess you already know that. She's such a wonderful flute player."

"Indeed she is. It's what I first fell in love with—the way she plays the flute." He put his arm around Jessica's waist and led her into the building.

She couldn't help but wonder what Karen had thought of his appearance—today's outfit was a hodgepodge of reds, oranges and greens—but actress that she was, Karen hadn't betrayed the slightest hint that there was anything out of the ordinary about him. Jessica wasn't so much embarrassed as amused to have to pass Griff off as her husband. Of course, if she'd really been married to him, she would have done something about those dreadful clothes—and about the haircut and stubble, too.

She excused herself to make the phone calls she'd planned to make earlier and then joined him in the audience. Their seats were on the aisle, about halfway back from the stage. As Karen had indicated, most of the performers were longer on ham than on talent, but the audience was encouraging and enthusiastic. Jessica was noticeably nervous by the time she and Karen took the stage. She was afraid their choice of song was all wrong—it was too serious and poignant.

Within seconds of the moment she began her introduction, a hush had fallen over the crowd. She'd more or less memorized her music and seldom looked at it. Instead, she divided her attention between Karen and the audience. She could feel the emotion in the room build and throb as the song continued. Everyone seemed to be caught up in it, even Griff.

He was staring so intently that Jessica wondered if the lyrics had some special meaning for him. Had there been missed opportunities in his life? Had he rejected somebody's love, only to realize months or years later that he cared—and that it was now too late?

Their eyes finally met, but he broke the contact almost at once. Jessica continued to scan the audience, trying to create an emotional bond with her listeners. It jarred her when she came to the one face that wasn't directed her way—to the one pair of eyes that wasn't watching the stage. The man was several rows in front of Griff, about ten seats in from the center aisle.

When he finally looked straight ahead, Jessica realized she'd seen him before. He'd come by her campsite when she was practicing under the trees, stopped for twenty or thirty seconds and then continued on his way. They hadn't spoken, but they'd exchanged a smile.

He looked to his right again, toward the center aisle, but Jessica had no way of knowing whom he was watching so curiously. A few seconds later she and Karen finished their song and the man's eyes swung back to the stage. The applause was loud and sustained, punctuated by cries of "Encore!" Karen smiled and asked Jessica how she felt about improvising another number. "Do you know 'Memory' from *Cats*?"

Jessica told her to name the key. She only hoped no comedians were scheduled to follow, because in its way, the song was as much of a tearjerker as "Send in the Clowns."

Jessica started first, giving Karen a short introduction. Again the audience quieted immediately, and again, Jessica caught Griff's eyes on her face. This time, she was the one who looked away first. His gaze affected her in a palpably physical way, making her pulse race and her face grow hot. She didn't understand these unpredictable flashes of attraction—not when the man treated her like part of the furniture most of the time, and not when his appearance was nothing short of outlandish.

Her admirer from the pine trees was still looking around, taking a furtive glance behind him every now and then in the direction of Jessica's empty seat. She wondered if he remembered her from this morning and was thinking about picking her up. He was thirtyish and nice looking, assuming you went for guys who were built like tanks. Jessica watched him for a moment longer and then turned her attention to Karen, who indicated that she should play a solo of the main theme.

After the piece was over they took their bows and briskly left the stage. Two little girls did a tap dance next, and were followed by the final act, a pianist playing Gershwin. Jessica's admirer took one last look toward her seat, but his face was stiff and hard this time. Puzzled and a little unnerved, she moved closer to Griff. It occurred to her that the man might be looking at *him*—that the two men might have met in the past. If so, Griff didn't seem to recognize him. Either he hadn't seen the man or didn't remember him.

Karen wrapped up the evening by thanking the audience for coming and then invited the performers and their families to join her in the lounge for dessert. Griff took full advantage of the occasion, going from person to person, asking about their backgrounds and what had brought them to Lake George. Jessica stayed by his side, listening carefully and trying to keep the different conversations straight. A couple from Kansas was showing their children the East. A family from New Jersey came here every year. A group of college students from Maine was travelling to Washington, D.C. It all seemed boringly prosaic, but Jessica was determined to remember every word and get it down on paper.

Back at the camper, Griff mumbled something about his aching knee and disappeared into his room. It was quite late, past eleven, and the campground was quiet. Jessica enjoyed this time of night, finding it peaceful and relaxing. She started working almost at once, making page after page of notes in her own personal shorthand.

She was concentrating so completely that the sound of somebody banging on the door sent her pencil flying out of her hand and straight up in the air. The banging continued as she walked to the door. "I know it's you, Marshall. Open the damn door!"

Jessica stood there, her eyes fixed on the lock. She wasn't about to open it, but maybe she could get a look at whoever was outside if she peeked through the side window. She crept up to it, taking care not to cast a shadow, and pushed back the curtain a little. She would have recognized that tanklike build anywhere.

The commotion was loud enough to disturb Griff, who looked half-asleep as he walked through the galley. "I recognize the man outside," Jessica told him. "He kept looking at you during the talent show. He seemed to be—angry about something. Did you notice him staring?"

Griff nodded. There was another spate of yelling punctuated by a hard, low thud—the sound of the man's boot crashing against the camper door. "His ex-wife was one of my students. He used to beat her up. I helped her leave and he hates me for it. I got a restraining order to keep him away from me in Massachusetts, but we're in New York now."

Jessica suddenly realized he meant to go outside and confront the man. She was so appalled that she grabbed his arm and tried to pull him backward. "You can't go out there, Griff. He's huge—the size of a football player. He'll kill you."

"What am I supposed to do? Let him destroy the camper?" The intruder was screaming Griff's name, daring him to come out and fight like a man. His voice was slurred, as if he'd been drinking. "I'll be okay. If he swings, I'll duck."

"But Griff—"

He pried loose her hands. "Wait inside, Jessica."

"But all that golf! You were so sore you could hardly move, and he's younger and stronger—"

He cut her off again, this time more firmly. "I said I'd be okay. Get away from the door."

Jessica stopped arguing. She was sure the intruder was going to beat Griff to a pulp, but she couldn't physically stop him if he was determined to go outside. Besides, there had been an aura of command in his voice that she was reluctant to challenge.

He turned the dead bolt and called out, "All right, O'Reilly. You want me—you've got me. Calm down and we'll talk about it."

The yelling finally stopped. Jessica watched through the window as Griff stepped outside and closed the camper door. O'Reilly cursed at him, then demanded, "Where is she? What did you do with her?"

"If she wanted to see you, she'd see you," Griff said. "She doesn't."

"My kid—"

"Which kid? The one you beat so badly he was in the hospital for three days?"

"I didn't do it. The jury said I was innocent." O'Reilly started forward, looking so menacing Jessica winced. A man who would beat his wife and child was capable of just about anything. "Where is she?" he demanded again.

Griff ignored the question. "The jury was hung, which isn't the same thing. You might have been able to use your political connections to avoid a second trial, but both of us know what the truth is." He turned to go back inside. "If you'll excuse me . . ."

O'Reilly bellowed another curse and charged like a wounded bull. Griff managed to sidestep him quickly enough to avoid the brunt of the blow, but he wasn't so lucky about O'Reilly's fist. It smashed into his back with enough force to make him stagger.

Jessica had seen enough. She ran through the camper and jumped outside through the driver's door, intent on finding somebody who could put a stop to this madness. The first people she noticed were a woman and a teenaged girl, both of whom were watching the fight from the middle of the access road. She recognized them as belonging to the family in the campsite across the street.

"My husband is looking for a security patrol," the woman called out. "Don't worry about your husband. He seems to be doing fine."

Much to Jessica's astonishment, it was true. O'Reilly was bigger and stronger, but he was also clumsy with drink. Although he'd knocked Griff's glasses off, he hadn't done any noticeable physical damage. He kept charging and swinging and Griff kept ducking out of the way.

Jessica was just telling herself that everything would be all right when O'Reilly changed the odds by pulling out a switchblade. One click and it was pointing at Griff's chest. Only six or seven feet separated the two men.

She instinctively started forward, but the woman from across the street pulled her back before she had taken more than a step. The next thing she knew, O'Reilly was throwing himself at Griff. Griff twisted to his right and swung his left arm. He landed a glancing blow off O'Reilly's jaw, and reached for his knife. O'Reilly recovered before Griff could manage to take it away.

They'd been fighting for only a few minutes but it seemed like hours. O'Reilly charged again, getting the knife so close to Griff's chest that Jessica was afraid he'd slashed Griff's shirt. Then, much to her astonishment, Griff grabbed O'Reilly's arm in a two-handed grip and executed what appeared to be a very expert judo takedown. O'Reilly lost his balance and started to fall, giving a ferocious kick against Griff's knee on the way down.

Jessica was terrified by what came next. She'd assumed Griff would get out of O'Reilly's way now that he'd knocked him down, but instead he threw himself on O'Reilly's body and reached for the knife again. It was impossible to tell who was winning—the two men were rolling around on the ground in the darkness, struggling over the knife. Jessica heard the sound of a security man's motor scooter and started shaking in relief.

Five seconds later the cop reached the campsite, but it was over by then. O'Reilly was on the ground, cursing and moaning in pain, and Griff was standing over him with the knife. Apparently the husband from across the street had filled the cop in, because he seemed to know exactly who had started things.

"I'll take that," he said to Griff, referring to the knife. "Are you all right, sir? We've got a doctor on call—"

"I'll be okay. It's just a few scratches." Griff explained what the fight was all about while O'Reilly stayed prone and silent. As he talked, he walked over to his glasses and put them back on. The security man asked Griff if he wanted to accompany him to the police station to press assault charges, but Griff shook his head. "Nobody really got hurt. I'd rather have him charged with drunk and disorderly conduct and stashed in jail for the night. I'll leave first thing in the morning, before he gets out."

The security man nodded and radioed the campground office to phone for a patrol car. Within minutes O'Reilly was on his way to the police station, the neighbors had gone to bed, and Jessica and Griff were locking their door for the night.

It wasn't until Jessica saw him in the light that she realized how badly hurt he was. At least it looked bad—his shirt was slashed to ribbons and stained with blood. She didn't even want to think about what had happened to his chest. He began to button up his sweater, hiding the damage from her eyes.

"You should see a doctor about that," she said. "The knife might have been dirty, you might need stitches—"

"The cuts aren't that deep," he interrupted. "I'll put some Neosporin on them."

Jessica gave him a skeptical look. "And when was your last tetanus shot?"

"Three years ago, *Dr.* Lawrence." His tone was so withering Jessica flushed, but she wasn't about to back down. "I don't need anyone to open my Band-Aids for me," he grumbled. "I'm not a five-year-old."

He started toward his room and Jessica followed, muttering, "You're certainly acting like one." She raised her voice. "I want to look at your chest, Griff. Superficial scratches don't bleed that much."

"Mine do." He stopped on the other side of the folding door and started to pull it closed. Jessica wasn't bold enough to follow him into the bathroom, but that didn't mean she'd given up. He couldn't stay in the bathroom forever.

She leaned against the kitchen counter, thinking about the fight she'd witnessed. Amazingly enough, O'Reilly had only kept the upper hand as long as Griff had refused to fight back. If O'Reilly hadn't had the knife, Griff would have dispatched him much sooner, and even with the knife, Griff had left him lying in the dirt. For a sociology professor who was sore from too much golf, he'd certainly known how to defend himself.

He was obviously a brave and compassionate man to involve himself in a student's life and help her free herself from an abusive husband. Jessica didn't doubt he had a host of good qualities, but he seldom allowed her to see any of them. Why not? Did he want her to think the worst of him?

She heard him leave the bathroom, walk into his bedroom, and pull the sliding door closed. There was a soft click—he'd turned the little knob that locked the door. It wasn't hard to open, though; all you had to do was press something flat against the edge of the door and run it up the side until the latch was pushed aside.

Ordinarily Jessica would never have considered such a thing, but she'd managed to convince herself that Griff was playing the macho hero and ignoring some serious wounds. Besides, she'd taken an excellent first-aid course the previous summer. Griff could be as sarcastic as he liked, but she was bound to know more about treating injuries than he did.

Steeling herself against the rough side of his tongue, she took out a carving knife and marched to his door. Within seconds she'd forced back the latch and was sliding the door open. Griff was sitting on the bed, turned away from her. His shirt was on his lap and his glasses and various medical supplies were sitting on the nightstand.

He put his glasses back on and picked up a packet of gauze. Then, still not looking at her, he ordered, "Out, Jessica. I'm fine. I don't need your help."

Jessica was so taken aback by the sight of his naked body that she almost obeyed without question. Those baggy shirts and sweaters had hidden muscular arms, a smooth, tan back and broad, powerful shoulders. Her mouth went dry. *That* was what she'd been sharing a camper with? A world-class hunk with the build of a professional athlete? Good grief!

She swallowed hard. "I'm not leaving until I check those cuts. Your macho orders don't impress me and neither does your sarcasm. If you need to see a doctor you're darn well going to see one, even if I have to help myself to your cycle and ride out to get him myself."

Griff turned around, giving Jessica her first good view of his chest. It more than matched the rest of him, especially in the rippling muscle department. Several fine scratches crisscrossed the flesh, oozing blood into the light scattering of hair.

"You're sure you're the same woman I interviewed last week?" he drawled.

. . . be tempted!

See inside for special
4 FREE BOOKS offer

Silhouette Romance™

Discover deliciously different romance with 4 Free Novels from

Silhouette Romance™

Sit back and enjoy four exciting romances—yours **FREE** from Silhouette Books! But wait . . . there's *even more* to this great offer! You'll also get . . .

A COMPACT MANICURE SET—ABSOLUTELY FREE! You'll love your beautiful manicure set—an elegant and useful accessory to carry in your handbag. Its rich burgundy case is a perfect expression of your style and good taste—and it's yours free with this offer!

PLUS A FREE MYSTERY GIFT— A surprise bonus that will delight you!

You can get all this just for trying Silhouette Romance!

FREE HOME DELIVERY!

Once you receive your 4 FREE books and gifts, you'll be able to preview more great romance reading in the convenience of your own home. Every month we'll deliver 6 brand-new Silhouette Romance novels right to your door months before they appear in stores. If you decide to keep them, they'll be yours for only $1.95 each—with no additional charges for home delivery!

SPECIAL EXTRAS—FREE!

You'll also get our monthly newsletter, packed with news of your favorite authors and upcoming books—FREE! And as a valued reader, we'll be sending you additional free gifts from time to time—as a token of our appreciation.

BE TEMPTED! COMPLETE, DETACH AND MAIL YOUR POSTPAID ORDER CARD TODAY AND RECEIVE 4 FREE BOOKS, A MANICURE SET AND A MYSTERY GIFT—PLUS LOTS MORE!

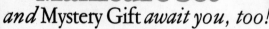

A FREE
Manicure Set
and Mystery Gift *await you, too!*

Clip and mail this postpaid card today!

Silhouette Romance™

Silhouette Books
901 Fuhrmann Blvd., P.O. Box 9013, Buffalo, NY 14240-9963

☐ **YES!** Please rush me my four Silhouette Romance novels with my FREE Manicure Set and Mystery Gift, as explained on the opposite page. I understand that I am under no obligation to purchase any books. The free books and gifts remain mine to keep.

215 CIL HAXG

NAME _____
(please print)

ADDRESS _____ APT. ____

CITY _____ STATE _____ ZIP _____

Offer limited to one per household and not valid for present subscribers.
Prices subject to change.

SILHOUETTE "NO-RISK" GUARANTEE

- There's no obligation to buy—and the free books and gifts remain yours to keep.
- You receive books before they appear in stores.
- You may end your subscription anytime—just write and let us know.

If offer card is missing, write to: Silhouette Books, 901 Fuhrmann Blvd., P.O. Box 9013, Buffalo, NY 14240-9013.

Jessica turned redder than ever. He was inspecting her as thoroughly as she'd inspected him, a clear reference to the way she'd looked and acted that day. "Of course I'm sure. It's just that I was soaked to the skin and I had a lot on my mind. My two uncles—but what's that got to do with your cuts?"

"Nothing, except I probably wouldn't have hired you if I'd known how bossy you were going to be. I wonder if Ulanoff realizes what he's getting into." He gestured toward the supplies on the nightstand. "I know when I'm licked, Miss Lawrence. Do what you want with my poor, battered body—but please, be gentle."

There wasn't a doubt in Jessica's mind that he was enjoying her embarrassment immensely. Obviously he realized she wasn't exactly a swinger. Women who slept around didn't blush at the sight of a bare male chest.

She sat down beside him, thinking she'd been a fool to assume he was oblivious to the opposite sex. Disheveled or not, he was a professor, and women considered professors very good catches. Plenty of them must have chased him, and more than a few must have caught up. And once they'd seen him with his clothes off... She forced herself to abandon that particular line of thought and attend to the task at hand.

The cuts weren't deep enough to need stitching, but they weren't surface scratches, either. Jessica was keenly aware of Griff's eyes on her face as she dabbed at his chest with peroxide. She could feel the heat of his body, smell the distinctive male scent of him. Unable to help herself, she sneaked a quick look at his face.

She wasn't an especially visual person so she couldn't picture him cleaned up, but the more she saw of him, the more convinced she was that he was actually quite attractive. In fact, without the glasses, stubble and uneven spikes of hair, he might have been downright handsome. She would have given the world to send him off to Elizabeth Arden for a total make-over.

She pursed her lips. There was something oddly magnetic about Griff, something that had affected her strongly from the start—negatively, it was true, but still strongly. She'd been quicker than usual to anger, quicker to protest, even quicker to forgive. Now she was sitting on his bed and tending to his wounds, all because she'd been as worried as a hen with her favorite chick. She'd shown a similar sort of devotion to her grandparents, of course, but it wasn't the same thing. Her body had never felt this hot when she'd tended to her grandparents' needs, and her hands had never shaken this way. Her stomach had never felt as if she'd swallowed a troupe of miniature acrobats, either.

She picked up the tube of Neosporin, squeezed a little onto her fingers, and rubbed it into his chest. He stiffened so abruptly that she rushed to apologize. "I'm sorry if it stings—"

"It doesn't sting." He smiled lazily. "You have a gentle touch—just what I'd expect from a flute player."

Jessica didn't answer. She knew he was teasing her again, that he'd spotted her physical reaction and found it amusing. She only wished she could have shared in the joke instead of feeling so miserably confused.

She'd never reacted to Alex this way, not even when he'd held her in his arms and comforted her. It seemed a little loose, somehow, a little cheap. She barely knew Griff Marshall, and even worse, she'd lectured him about sexual harassment. What kind of woman was she, to sit here fantasizing about the most shockingly unprofessional things?

She squeezed another dab of ointment onto her fingers and raised them to his chest. The cuts were still oozing a little, staining the Neosporin red. "You should cover those scratches up," she said, "but the hair on your chest—if I use tape and gauze it's going to hurt when you take it off. A clean undershirt might be better."

"They're in the wardrobe," he said. "In the top drawer."

Jessica had assumed he would go for the shirt himself, not expect her to wait on him. Was he teasing her again? Deliberately goading her? Or simply tired and in pain? He wasn't smiling anymore, so perhaps it was the last.

He sat there placidly watching as she fetched the shirt, only smiling again when she held it out. "You mean you're not going to dress me, too?" he asked.

That was when Jessica knew she'd been had. He *had* been making fun of her. "You can do it yourself," she said, annoyed with herself for falling for it.

"I could have done *all* of it myself. It wasn't exactly major surgery." He took the shirt out of her hands. "Of course, if I had, you probably would have spent a sleepless night telling yourself I was bleeding to death in my bed. Do you worry about everyone this way or should I be flattered?"

"I'm not used to seeing people get stabbed." Jessica raised her chin, openly angry now. "You might at least thank me for being concerned. The way you act, it's like I was trying to torture you."

"You made a terrific Florence Nightingale." He pulled on his shirt. "I'm eternally grateful. Now get out of here and take all this junk with you."

Jessica turned to the nightstand and busied herself with gathering up the various packages. She was hurt and couldn't hide it. What did it take to please this man and why did she even bother? He was an ill-mannered ingrate, not worth her time or trouble.

She wasn't expecting him to speak again, much less touch her, so when his hand came down on her shoulder she flinched violently. "Thank you for your concern," he said softly. "It's probably more than I deserve." For once there was no sarcasm in his voice. He actually seemed to mean it.

Her emotions had skittered all over the map during the past half hour and she had no defenses left. She turned to face him, her hands full of medical supplies, and gazed into his eyes. She wanted to make some clever retort about his finally learning some manners, but nothing would come out. His eyes were too gentle, his face too solemn.

He ran his finger lightly down her cheek. It was a brotherly caress, but her skin got warmer and her pulse began to race. It was crazy, but she wanted him to hold her. No, not just hold her—kiss her. She took a small step forward and murmured his name. Her desire couldn't have been any more obvious if she'd spoken it aloud.

"You're a sweet kid," he said, and yawned. "You've had a rough night. Go get some sleep." He gave her a pat on the head, sat down on the bed, and proceeded to ignore her.

Mortified, Jessica nodded and hurried out of the room. Was there no end to the humiliation she was destined to suffer at his hands? Not only did he consider her inept, he thought of her as a child. Her job was beginning to seem like a long, unbroken string of disasters.

Chapter Eight

Griff would have liked to spend the next few weeks in his room, only emerging on August fifteenth when it was time to take Jessica back to Boston. Nothing had gone right on this case. First he'd run into Joe O'Reilly, a piece of left-over trouble from another one of his cases who was unpleasant sober and scum when he was drunk, and then O'Reilly had come looking for a fight. Even worse, he'd started waving around a knife, forcing Griff to defend himself a damn sight too capably for your average sociology professor. He hadn't wanted to arouse Jessica's suspicions so he'd barely fought back at first, and what was his reward? A chestful of scratches.

The scratches, of course, had provided the crowning screwup to the whole evening. Griff could hardly believe that Ulanoff had characterized Jessica as timid and tractable. In her own quiet way, the lady was a human bulldozer. Nothing stopped her—not curtness, not sarcasm, not even locked doors. Griff was still incredulous at the way she'd barged into his room. Never in a million years had he expected her to be so bold, not when the mere thought of sharing a trailer with a man had once sent her into paroxysms of maidenly modesty. When she took it into her head to worry, she didn't fool around.

Even a solid night's sleep hadn't dimmed the memory of her fingers on his chest. She'd touched him the same way she touched her flute—delicately, gently, exquisitely. It had aroused the hell out of him, but even being in the same room with her aroused him. And when she gazed at him with her lips slightly parted and her eyes glazed with desire . . .

He shook his head impatiently and got out of bed. Seducing an innocent like Jessica Lawrence was about as moral as seducing Snow White. There was no point fantasizing about it. There were certain givens to this case, and if he had any brains, he would keep them in mind.

Not only did he have to keep Jessica away from Boston for the next several weeks; he had to make sure nothing happened to her. If the past three days were any indication, she was headstrong and volatile. If she ever found out she'd been set up she would hightail it home and give Ulanoff hell, but first she would lace into *him*. That was reason enough to keep her in the dark. Every time she scolded him, he wanted to pull her into his arms and shut her up.

The trailer was still completely quiet, so apparently she hadn't gotten up yet. Griff wanted to be sure she'd be wearing a robe before he came out, so he made as much noise as possible as he showered and dressed. The outfit he chose was one of his favorites, a hideous collection of garments he'd discovered at a suburban garage sale. The shirt was olive green, a color that made him look as if he'd eaten some bad fish, and was decorated with all sorts of silly hardware—buckles, snaps and studs. The pants were pink with mud-brown wavy stripes, held up by brown suspenders. He was especially creative with his can of silver spray, highlighting his hair just so and rubbing a little coloring on the artful stubble he maintained with a special razor he'd bought in the days when looking like a bum had been considered sexy.

Checking himself in the mirror, he decided that Jessica's gain was Hollywood's loss. He could have been one of the all-time great costume designers, no question about it.

He could hear her in the kitchen now, putting away last night's dishes. Since her previous reluctance to question him probably wouldn't last much longer, he took a moment to plan his answers. If she asked about his scratches, he would show them to her. It was better to satisfy her curiosity than to arouse it by stonewalling her. If she asked about O'Reilly, he would bill himself as a good samaritan rather than admitting the truth—that he'd been hired by O'Reilly's father-in-law to check on whether O'Reilly was being faithful. Late one night, Griff had seen O'Reilly beating his wife and child and had charged in to stop him. Within a few weeks, he was helping them start a new life.

Finally, if Jessica asked about her job, he would say they'd be conducting interviews at their next campsite. He could only get away with so many days of golf.

He put on his glasses, messed up his hair, and steeled himself for another day in the field.

Griff needn't have worried, because the last thing Jessica wanted to do was ask questions. The dull feeling in the pit of her stomach reminded her only too forcefully that her curiosity had led to disaster the night before. She would have liked to forget he even existed.

She avoided him at first, waiting until he'd gone into his room to dress before she even got up. Luck was with her for once, because he wasn't in the camper when she finally left the bathroom. And when he returned, he was as unsociable as ever.

Given how embarrassed she was, his silence was a godsend. The quiet breakfast they shared gave her a chance to put things in perspective. In fact, by the time she cleared away the dishes, everything about the night before had taken on a dreamlike glow.

Rationally she knew that Griff's execrable olive shirt covered the body of a linebacker, but she couldn't quite bring herself to believe it. Between worry and exhaustion, surely she'd seen more than was there. As for his looks, he would have been attractive if somebody had cleaned him up, but there was nothing especially compelling about him. Far from experiencing the overwhelming attraction of the night before, she felt only normal human concern.

Even so, she'd been burned and burned badly. She was wary enough of further humiliation that it took her until they were packed and on their way to even ask him how he was feeling. He answered that he was fine, and then, to Jessica's astonishment, elaborated almost chattily. "There's no sign of infection. The cuts stung a little when I took a shower this morning, but they didn't bleed. There's no reason to worry."

"I'll try not to." Jessica paused, then admitted, "I don't think I've ever been so frightened as when O'Reilly took out that knife. It never occurred to me that you could defend yourself that way. Most professors don't know judo."

"'Mens sana in corpore sano,'" he quoted, and when Jessica gave him a blank look, translated, "A sound mind in a sound body. I got interested in martial arts while I was in Asia, researching my book on the Japanese work ethic."

Jessica hadn't heard of the book and couldn't think of anything intelligent to say about it, so she changed the subject. "Did your training ever come in handy before?"

"Only with Joe O'Reilly." He launched into an involved story about Joe and his ex-wife Anne, who'd married him when she was seventeen and had gradually outgrown him. She was remarried now, living in Michigan, and was studying to become a psychologist.

The story completed, he lapsed back into silence. They were traveling north on 87 and Jessica wondered where they were going. The last time she'd asked about their destination he'd practically bitten her head off, but this time he was close to effusive. "Grand Isle in Lake Champlain. We'll catch the ferry at Plattsburgh. It's another sixty miles or so. Everything was pretty crowded, but I was lucky. One of the campgrounds had a last-minute cancellation for the next five nights."

Jessica wanted to suggest that they map out the rest of their itinerary as soon as possible and send in the appropriate deposits, but Griff had a habit of getting annoyed at the most unpredictable things. Besides, she realized that a lot of people were more spontaneous than she was, and that too much planning spoiled their fun.

They reached their Grand Isle campground late that morning. It had a swimming pool, playground, general store and recreation room, but there were no elaborate buildings and facilities like the ones at Lake George. Their site was right beside Lake Champlain, an idyllic spot within easy walking distance of a dock where small fishing boats could be rented. About half the other sites were occupied by people in tents, so the general feel of the place was less affluent. Jessica's instincts told her this would be a better place to conduct their research than the luxurious all-trailer campground at Lake George. The people here were more typical of average American vacationers.

They spent the afternoon settling in. Jessica cleaned house and did laundry while Griff motorcycled into the nearest town, South Hero, for food and supplies. When he got back he announced rather grandly that he would cook dinner that night, creating a stir-fried Chinese dish with enough ginger in it to clear one's sinuses for a month. The fact that it wasn't perfect pleased Jessica no end. She even teased him that if he complained about her cooking again he would never hear the end of the ginger.

Griff went into his room to work on his lectures afterward and Jessica sat down to practice. As the evening wore on, she began to fret about his scratches. Were they healing as well as he'd claimed? Suppose he was acting the martyr again?

Within minutes she was standing by his door, only this time she had the good sense to knock rather than break in. He didn't give her an argument about taking off his shirt, just shrugged, pulled it over his head and tossed it aside. He hadn't lied about the scratches—they were much less red and swollen. Unfortunately, her memory hadn't lied about his body, either. It was bone-meltingly gorgeous.

He waited a few seconds and then reached for his shirt. "Satisfied?" he drawled.

"Yes." Jessica glanced at the yellow legal pad on his bed as he dressed. His notes covered the entire page, with several other pages flipped over and tucked behind. His handwriting was barely legible, just what one would expect from somebody who seemed constitutionally incapable of tidiness.

"How is your work coming?" she asked. "My playing isn't disturbing you again, is it?"

"Distracting me, maybe, but not disturbing me. It's hard to concentrate on the sociological implications of the technologizing of the workplace when someone is playing— who's the composer? Bach, maybe?"

"Yes. His Suite No. 2 in B Minor." Jessica was surprised he'd known. He always tuned in Top 40 stations when they traveled. "I should let you get back to your lectures—"

"No, wait. I could use a break." He paused. "How about having a cup of coffee with me? We should decide on the rest of our itinerary. I had this vision of total freedom—of coming and going on the spur of the moment—but this camper isn't exactly a pup tent. Most places don't have hookups, or if they do, they're all booked up." He smiled sheepishly. "So much for my middle-aged fantasies."

"It's got nothing to do with age. Look at me. If the choice is between comfort and spontaneity, I'll take comfort every time." Jessica would have liked to add that the only thing middle-aged about Griff was his eccentric appearance, but their relationship didn't include making such personal remarks. She offered to heat the coffee instead.

By the time she'd brought the coffee to the table, Griff had fetched their maps and guidebooks and was spreading them out in front of him. After a minute or two of trying to read them upside down, Jessica left her seat across from him and sat down beside him. The feeling she'd had at first, of being comfortably in tune with him, gave way to uneasiness. She couldn't seem to forget the power in his body, the graceful way he moved, or how expertly he could defend himself. The parts of her that didn't tingle, ached.

She told herself it was nothing but raw attraction—to forget it and move on. Alex was closer to her ideal, wasn't he? Charm, culture, sophistication, kindness—he had them all. He knew everyone who mattered in Boston, he dressed beautifully and his manners were impeccable. She was lucky he wanted to marry her.

Of course, Griff could be charming, too, when he put his mind to it. He could even be kind, and certainly he was brilliant. It was only natural to feel some sort of attraction

to him, especially when they spent day after day in each
other's company. He probably could have been anyone and
she would have felt the same way.

She stared at the map of Vermont and New Hampshire,
not really seeing it. The explanation made sense, especially
to a woman who'd never lived close to any man other than
her grandfather. It was also more comfortable than admitting that Griff might have the potential to turn her life upside down.

"What do you think about the White Mountains?" he
asked. "We could try the Woodstock area. There's some
beautiful country around there."

Jessica didn't really care where they went. What mattered was that he'd consulted her. "It sounds wonderful.
I've always wanted to go fishing. You can teach me how."
She grinned at him. "I'll catch, you clean and cook. After
all, you're so much better with food than I am."

"Why do I have the feeling I'm being manipulated into
doing all the work?" He turned the map over. "The White
Mountains it is, then. How about the Maine coast? Ever
been there?"

"To Bar Harbor, once," Jessica said. "I loved it."

"We could go there for a week or so and then stop near
Portland. I have a cousin I'd like to visit." He stretched his
arms over his head, yawning. "I'm going to turn in, Jessica. I don't have the energy I used to, and we need to put in
a full day's work tomorrow. Play something soft and
soothing, okay?"

The piece Jessica chose, Mozart's Andante in C Major,
was as melodic and soothing as anyone could wish. She was
relaxed and sleepy by the time she finished playing, and went
to bed not long after Griff did.

She'd never seen a sociologist at work, but a day of ob-
serving Griff in action taught her that successful research

was largely a matter of dealing well with one's subjects. Amazingly enough, the same Griff Marshall who'd driven her batty with his unresponsiveness and condescension was superb at drawing people out.

It was amusing, really. Strangers kept their distance at first, probably because Griff was dressed so oddly, but it never took long for them to warm to his charm. He would tell them he was a computer scientist and mumble some technical mumbo jumbo, and they would nod in acceptance. Scientists, it seemed, were expected to look eccentric.

Jessica became quite proficient as the days passed, but still couldn't see the point of it. So what if Mr. and Mrs. Quiller's heart-shaped bed had collapsed while they were honeymooning in the Poconos, wrenching Mr. Quiller's back and getting their marriage off to a terrible start? Did it matter that the Osbornes from Utah had been mugged while on vacation in Chicago or that the Rices from Kansas had had car trouble in western New York? The Goldmans' kids always fought like cats and dogs while the Mazellis had never taken a trip that wasn't perfect, but who cared? Did the summer holidays of the Anthony and Marie Mazellis of this world win academic prizes for professors or contribute to a better understanding of human society? Jessica doubted it, but she continued to do her job as best she could.

A comfortable pattern developed. After working all morning, Jessica would return to the camper while Griff ran errands in town. She would make some notes and then practice until he got back. More interviews followed. Although Griff always cooked breakfast, they took turns fixing dinner. In the evenings he would work on his lectures while Jessica wrote up the day's conversations and practiced a bit more.

Their itinerary wound up pretty much as they'd planned, except that they had to put Bar Harbor after Portland in order to get reservations there. With everything settled, Jessica called Mrs. MacPherson and then Alex with a list of campground names and dates. Mrs. MacPherson was delighted things were working out so well, remarking that she was thinking of visiting her daughter in Seattle. Jessica told her to go on the trip and stay as long as she liked.

As for Alex, Jessica felt a little guilty when she spoke to him, a little disloyal. It wasn't honest to go on and on about how eccentric Griff could be without also mentioning that he was charming, amusing and kind. It was even less honest to hide the fact that she was attracted to him, and, perhaps because of that, intensely and increasingly curious about him.

First and foremost, she didn't understand the change in his personality. He was still distant much of the time, but never curt or condescending. Why the drastic improvement? And why the strange choice of research topics? It seemed rather frivolous given his brilliant reputation. She didn't understand the way he looked and dressed, either. He wasn't some ivory-tower academic—his work had taken him all over the country and even to Europe and Asia. He'd interviewed prominent, polished people. Surely he must have noticed how *they* looked and dressed, so why the tasteless clothes? Why the awful haircut? Sometimes she thought it was some sort of disguise, adopted as part of his role as a computer scientist, but if so, why would he keep playing it in private? Was she right that he was conducting an experiment that she was an unwitting part of?

By the weekend her suspicions had begun to consume her. They even extended to minor details like his glasses. He wore them all the time, but did he really need them? Now that she thought about it, he evidently locked them away at night.

Certainly they hadn't been on his nightstand the evening she'd played the flute in his room. Was he purposely hiding them?

And what about the fight with O'Reilly? The glasses had either been knocked off or deliberately removed, but Griff hadn't seemed to miss them. Surely one couldn't execute complicated judo moves or take away somebody else's knife if everything was a blur.

The glasses preyed on Jessica's mind until they'd turned into a key—a key that would unlock the door to the real Griff Marshall. If only she could get him to take them off, if only she could look through them, she would finally discover the truth.

She wasn't the type of person who looked for convoluted solutions to problems, so she tried the most direct approach first. At dinner on Sunday she remarked as artlessly as she could that she'd spoken to Alex that day and he was quite put out because his ophthalmologist had prescribed reading glasses. "He thinks he's too young for them, but everybody seems to need them eventually," she said, embroidering on a story she'd invented out of whole cloth. "How about you? Have you always worn glasses?"

"Since I was a child," he answered. "I have a bad case of astigmatism."

"So everything looks blurry if you don't wear them?"

Griff nodded. Jessica promptly asked to try them on, saying she'd always been curious about people's prescriptions, but he flatly refused. "I don't like other people to touch them," he said.

Jessica waited for an explanation of this strange hang-up but none was forthcoming. If she wanted to look through his glasses she would have to do it without permission, but how was that possible when he wore them every moment of the day and locked them up at night?

She brooded about it all through dinner. Surely he didn't wear them in the shower. If she forced the lock on the bathroom door, she could dart inside for a quick look. Unfortunately, the shower stall door was clear glass, so she'd get a look at a lot more of Griff than his glasses. She reluctantly rejected the plan. She was far too shy to be blasé about ogling a naked man, and besides, Griff might spot her and realize she was up to something. Suppose her imagination was running away with her and he was exactly what he claimed? She'd made a fool of herself too many times already to risk doing it again.

That left only one alternative—to unlock his nightstand while he was sleeping. She'd noticed that he threw his trousers over a wooden clothes valet at night, probably with the keys still in his pocket. How hard could it be to creep in with her pencil flashlight, retrieve the keys, and unlock the nightstand? She would even get to see what else he kept in there.

It was a good plan, but nighttime came and went without her carrying it out. Suppose he woke up and caught her redhanded? What could she possibly say?

Fortunately she had a fertile mind and soon came up with another plan of attack. She and Griff had talked about going fishing but hadn't gotten around to it yet. She could convince him to rent a boat and take her out, then suggest a dip in the lake. Nobody swam with their glasses on. If she could beat him back to the boat, she could look through the glasses while he was still in the water. He might never notice.

The plan worked perfectly, at least at first. Griff agreed to go fishing and even dressed for the water, putting on a crimson T-shirt and a pair of long, baggy trunks decorated with huge, bright flowers. Jessica was dressed more conservatively in a black and yellow maillot she'd bought before leaving Boston. It had been a little big then, but hugged her body like a second skin now.

Maybe it was because she was wearing so little herself, but she was more aware of Griff than ever. His legs—what she could see of them—were as muscular as the rest of him, and his baggy T-shirt couldn't hide the power in his chest and arms as he rowed the boat. It was impossible to watch him and still keep her mind on fishing.

When it got to the point where she couldn't tell whether she was feverish from the hot sun or her own overactive imagination, she put down her fishing rod and dove off the boat. Treading and shivering in the cold water, she called out, "It feels great! Why don't you come in?"

He gave her an apologetic look. "I'd like to, but I should wait. My chest is still sore."

Jessica was positive he was lying. Four days had gone by, plenty of time for him to heal. Even so, she couldn't very well tell him he didn't know the condition of his own body. She swam for another minute, and then, blue-lipped, climbed back into the boat. Another scheme had gone down to defeat.

The repeated failures left her frustrated and out-of-sorts. It should have been easy to get a look through someone's glasses, but Griff continually outmaneuvered her. He had to be hiding something. If only she'd had the guts to snatch them off his face—but she didn't. He'd probably duck out of reach before she could grab them, then demand to know what her problem was.

She was too restless to sleep soundly that night, waking repeatedly until, at two in the morning, she finally gave up and got out of bed. Griff seemed to be dead to the world—she could hear him snoring. The hard truth was that she'd run out of alternatives. She would have to steal the keys.

Her heart was beating double time as she approached his door. Carving knife in hand, she forced aside the lock. It made the same soft click as before, but this time it sounded as loud as a hammer striking metal to her ears. She slid the door aside, wincing at the way it creaked.

There were windows on three sides of the room and a three-quarter moon outside, but the curtains were drawn against the light and Jessica had trouble making out the furniture. She stood and listened, letting her eyes adapt to the darkness. Griff was still snoring gently, apparently fast asleep.

She tiptoed a few feet into the room and turned on her pencil flashlight. Just as she'd expected, he'd tossed his trousers and also a sweater over the wooden valet to the left of the bed. Griff grunted and changed position as she crept over to it, sending her blood pressure soaring. She turned off her flashlight and waited, fighting the urge to flee. Other than the soft sound of his breathing, everything was silent and still.

Using her body to block the beam of light, she turned on the flashlight and shone it on his trousers. All four pockets were empty. The same was true of the pockets in his sweater. No keys, no wallet, no change. Where had he put everything?

He seemed to be a heavy sleeper, so she took a chance on walking around to his wardrobe. There was another click as the latch disengaged, but no change in the pattern of Griff's breathing. Jessica checked all the drawers, quickly feeling their contents, but discovered only clothing and books.

Her body was taut with frustration now. There were three overhead bins in this room, stuffed with everything from extra blankets to an emergency tool kit. Even assuming she could search them without waking Griff up, it would take forever to check all the nooks and crannies where he might have tucked a set of keys.

She was about to give up when she realized she'd forgotten the most obvious move of all—she hadn't checked that the nightstand was actually locked. Griff was no more than two feet away as she bent down beside it; he lay on his back, breathing deeply and a little irregularly. She pressed in the latch that held the drawer in place and pulled hard, but nothing happened. The same was true of the door below. He *had* locked the nightstand.

She was still kneeling there, cursing her rotten luck, when Griff rolled onto his side. That was when she heard it—the soft but unmistakable tingle of metal keys shifting and colliding. She took a quick deep breath, half-triumphant, half-terrified. Good grief, the keys were in his pocket! When he turned onto his stomach, moving to the far side of the bed, she heard the unmistakable tinkle again.

Did she dare try to steal them? She'd made a fair amount of noise, but Griff seemed to be sleeping just as soundly as before. Could she remove them without waking him?

She was debating the pros and cons when Griff rolled onto his back again. Jessica decided it was a sign from the gods. If the powers that be hadn't wanted her to succeed, they wouldn't have made the keys so temptingly accessible.

She eased back the covers and slid onto the bed. Squinting in the darkness—she could barely see but didn't dare use her flashlight—she felt for the pocket on Griff's pajama top. It was flat, empty.

She took a deep breath, raised her hand, and moved it slowly downward. She was bending over Griff's body now, her hair spilling onto his chest. His trousers were even harder to see than his jacket, so her only option was to probe with her fingers until she felt the set of keys. Her heart was beating so fiercely she never noticed that Griff's breathing was no longer heavy and irregular. She dropped her hand to his hip, realized she'd placed it too far over, and, mortified, yanked it away.

Before she had a chance to recover, a hard male arm snaked across her belly and curved around her waist. She jerked away in shock, but Griff tightened his grip to prevent her from leaving. She had no idea if he was awake enough to realize what he was doing. Maybe he thought she was an intruder.

There was nothing she could say, no way she could justify her presence, so she sat absolutely motionless and prayed he would fall back asleep. Instead he pulled himself up so that his chest was flush against her back and settled his lips against the nape of her neck. Her heart was still beating frantically, but not just from shock or fear. A part of her was dying for this.

He found the sash at her waist and untied it, then pushed aside her robe and burrowed underneath. She started to tremble as he repeatedly brushed the undersides of her breasts with the back of his hand. The teasing delicacy of his touch was fogging her mind, making it impossible to think. Never in her life had she felt such intense excitement—or such a melting need to submit.

She rolled her head forward, allowing his lips to roam where they pleased. She felt them on her shoulder, and then, as he pulled her around and took her in his arms, nuzzling their way to her throat.

"I love the way you smell," he murmured. His tongue was against her throat. "And the way you taste." His mouth moved higher, to her chin, and her lips began to burn for his possession.

She parted them expectantly. "Griff, please..."

"Relax. It's okay." His mouth settled on hers, moving lightly and erotically against her lips. Jessica wound her arms around his neck and tried to catch her breath. There didn't seem to be enough air in the room. He kept tasting and teasing, exploring the corners of her mouth and the outline of her lips, but she wanted—needed—more. Finally, when her body was pressed tensely against his and her hands were clenched around his neck in frustration, he gave her what she'd been wanting from the very beginning.

Weak with pleasure, Jessica let him do as he wished. In some far corner of her mind she knew this was crazy—decent young women didn't climb into bed with their bosses and beg for such deep, intimate kisses—but it didn't seem to matter. His mouth and touch were like something out of an intoxicating dream.

But the dream turned into a nightmare with mortifying abruptness. Yawning, Griff buried his lips against her neck and mumbled, "Roxy—sweetheart—I'm so tired." His body went limp against hers. "So tired." His voice was slurred with sleep now. "Stay with me."

Somehow Jessica managed to stay in his bed until he'd lain back down and fallen into a light sleep. Then she hurried out of his room as though all the hounds of hell were nipping at her bare heels.

Chapter Nine

Griff figured he had two choices. First, he could level with Jessica completely and admit he'd known exactly whom he was making love to the night before. True, he'd been a little hazy at first—so hazy his desire had overwhelmed his common sense—but he didn't regret a moment of it. He didn't feel guilty, either, not after what Roxy had told him about Jessica's would-be fiancé.

For a man who professed to be in love, Ulanoff led a very active social life. Early in the week, Roxy had trailed him to the theater and seen him leave with a notoriously promiscuous actress, and then, two nights later, watched him enter a private gambling club with a high-living socialite. It was safe to assume that neither of these evenings had ended with a polite handshake. In Griff's opinion, his own intentions toward Jessica were more honorable than Ulanoff's. Whereas Ulanoff would wait until they were married to sleep with her but then cheat like hell, Griff would have seduced her without a qualm if he'd been ready to make a commitment. He wasn't ready to do any such thing yet, but his feelings were far from casual. If desire, protectiveness and pleasure in her company had anything to to with falling in love, he was falling hard.

According to Roxy, Jessica was surrounded by a rogues' gallery of eccentrics and scoundrels. Her Uncle Ernest, while honest, was pathologically attached to Lawrence Shoes and would have sold his soul to the devil in order to stay in charge. Unlike Ernest, her Uncle Charles was receptive to a little larceny as long as he didn't get caught. It was his dearest wish to sell Lawrence Shoes and live happily ever after off the profits, and what chicanery he might resort to in order to bring this about was anybody's guess.

Ernest's daughter, Emily, was cut from the same tiresomely upstanding cloth as her father, as was Ron Chase, Emily's fiancé. Charles' sons, however, were most charitably described as rank opportunists. Charles Jr., known as Chuck, was a brilliant law student who'd made no secret of the fact that he intended to make a bundle someday protecting the interests of huge corporations. His younger brother, Todd, was the black sheep of the family, a likable but irresponsible college student who'd been bailed out of minor scrapes more times than his father probably cared to remember. According to Roxy, Todd had a dismaying affinity for fraternity pranks, gambling and fast cars.

Griff was more than a little worried about these people, seeing them as self-serving and potentially dangerous. He didn't want Jessica within a hundred miles of them. Unfortunately, that precluded telling her the truth. She was much too proper to travel around in a camper with a man who wasn't her husband unless it was part of some legitimate job. If he leveled with her, she would only lose her temper, suffer fits of embarrassment, and run back to that den of thieves in Boston.

That left only one alternative—out-and-out deception. Griff's instincts told him it was the right way to go—had been telling him that since the moment he'd deliberately called Jessica "Roxy" and pretended to fall dead asleep. He was only grateful that his common sense had reasserted itself while he'd still had the wit to stop.

He wasn't sure what she'd been doing in his bed in the first place but imagined it had something to do with his glasses, which she seemed determined to wrest from his face. He kept them in the bin over his bed at night, but maybe she'd thought they were locked in the nightstand and had been searching for the keys. He couldn't figure out how she'd known the keys were in his pajama pocket, but no other explanation made sense.

For a man who'd always insisted he could talk his way out of anything, Griff felt uncharacteristically stymied. He knew that Jessica had a strong sense of loyalty toward Ulanoff. As heatedly as she'd responded to his lovemaking, she was obviously no femme fatale. He had no idea how he could convince her to stay on as his "research assistant" when she was probably so embarrassed by her behavior that all she wanted to do was run away.

As Griff had assumed, Jessica was suffering the torments of the damned. Her grandmother had reserved a special scorn for girls who were "fast" or "loose," and she was sure she'd tumbled into both despicable categories. Alex trusted her completely, and she'd betrayed him with another man. She couldn't blame Griff for that, only herself. *He'd* been half-asleep and under the impression she was somebody named Roxy, but *she'd* known exactly what she was doing. Surely he'd realized by now that she'd been the woman in his bed, and that she'd allowed him the most appalling liberties. The humiliation was going to be excruciating.

She couldn't even bring herself to look at him when he walked out of his room that morning. Eyes downcast, she started toward the bathroom to take her turn in the shower.

"I have a headache," he said curtly. "*You* can make breakfast for once. Call me when it's ready." Jessica looked up as he pulled the bedroom door closed.

She didn't know what she'd expected, but it wasn't a display of rudeness to rival the worst moments of their first day together. Startled and a little annoyed, she made her way to the bathroom. No sooner had she showered and dressed than he started yelling at her. "What the hell is taking you so long? I'm hungry!"

She made a face at his door as she walked to the galley. What was his problem? Frustration? Was she supposed to have stayed in his room all night and serviced him come morning?

She put some sausage into a fry pan and took out some eggs. Now that she thought about it, he was probably angry that she'd broken into his room. Guilty and chastened, she concentrated on preparing breakfast. It wasn't one of her better efforts—she cooked the scrambled eggs too long, by which time the toast had gotten cold.

Griff, unfortunately, was in no mood to tolerate mistakes. The meals he'd suffered in silence were delights compared to this one. He even muttered sarcastic comments under his breath: "What were you trying to do to the toast? Freeze-dry it?" and "These eggs aren't scrambled—they're petrified."

Jessica's resentment simmered and grew, finally boiling over when he shoved away his plate in distaste. "So I'm a rotten cook!" she said. "I'm sorry, okay? If you want me to leave—"

"Leave?" He stared down his nose at her. "Who's going to write up my notes if you leave?"

"You are," she answered. "It's obvious you're angry—"

"I'm not angry. I have a bad headache. I'm in a lousy mood. You don't have to take it so personally."

"How else am I supposed to take it when it's obviously because of last night?" Jessica blurted out. Then she bit her lip, appalled with herself. She'd wanted to avoid the subject.

"You have to practice the damn exercises some time—I understand that and I accept it. Did I complain?" he demanded.

Jessica blinked at him. Did he really think she'd been talking about a bunch of music exercises? "Well, no," she said. "That is, I thought—you and I—last night..." Her voice trailed off. It was too excruciating to go on.

She was sitting there in silent agony when he did the quickest about-face she'd ever seen. "Oh, hell, Jessica, I'm sorry. This damn headache is driving me up the wall, but I have no right to take it out on you." He gave her a weak smile. "I can't even blame it on MSG, since *I* cooked the fish last night. I was awake for what seemed like hours, and then when I finally fell asleep, I must have tossed and turned half the night. I had the craziest dreams—none of them made sense."

"Dreams?" Jessica squeaked. Did he actually think he'd been dreaming?

"Yes. There's a woman in my department—" He shook his head, visibly embarrassed. "Never mind. I'm going to get some ice for my head and lie down. We're supposed to check out by eleven, but I'm in no shape to drive yet."

"I could play for you," Jessica offered hesitantly. He seemed to be in such pain that it tore at her heart.

He smiled again, more warmly this time. "I'd like that."

Not only did she play—she massaged his neck and back until he dropped off to sleep, and later, when he'd gotten up, insisted on doing the driving. The trailer was a monster, but it handled surprisingly easily. Besides, there was very little traffic.

Their campground was located in the White Mountains, surrounded on all sides by national forest. With so much beauty all around and miles of tranquil, isolated country to explore, Jessica had no desire to practice. She and Griff wound up taking a long hike, not talking very much but comfortable in each other's company.

It was bewildering, really. Even if Griff couldn't remember what had happened, Jessica did. The knowledge of what she'd done should have embarrassed her, but it didn't. She could only assume she'd managed to put Griff in the same category as her grandparents. Having taken care of him several times, she saw him as somebody to look after and care for—not a relative whom she loved dearly, of course, but a good friend.

The friendship got deeper and more intimate over the next several days, but it happened so gradually that Jessica scarcely noticed. She and Griff took to lingering over their meals, spending as much time talking as working. Books, movies, politics, Boston society—Griff would discuss any topic she chose, only avoiding anything too private. She knew men tended to be reticent about their pasts and didn't press him. He seemed interested in her own life, asking her question after question, and she found it easy to open up to him. By Thursday he knew everything: how she'd been raised by her grandparents after her parents had died in an accident; how Alex had grown increasingly close to the family during her grandparents' final years until she couldn't imagine how she would have coped without him; how she was caught in a fight between two uncles who used every appeal and threat in the book to get her to vote their way. Far from thinking her weak or irresponsible, he was sympathetic and supportive. He advised her to let her uncles battle it out without her, saying that the way they'd behaved, they deserved whatever they did to each other.

All in all, Jessica was happy with the status quo. She was no less curious than before, but they were getting along so well she was reluctant to risk questioning him. Every now and then she would look at him and feel the same overpowering attraction she'd felt on Grand Isle, but she ignored it as best she could. He seemed to be infatuated with this Roxy person while she still had Alex to think of. Although she was beginning to realize she would never love Alex the way a woman should love her husband, she felt it would be kinder to tell him so in person. Then she could get on with her life.

Griff being Griff, he threw a monkey wrench into her safe little world by the simple act of walking out of his bathroom clean-shaven. Not only did he look years younger, he had the cutest dimples she'd ever seen and a smile that lit up the room. It was getting harder and harder to think of him only as a friend.

"You have no idea how good it feels to shave," he remarked. "I was having a problem with my skin—some kind of allergy—and the dermatologist told me to lay off the regular razor for a while. I've hated every day of it—the only thing worse than stubble is a beard."

"If I'd seen the real you—" Jessica smiled and blushed. She'd gotten into the habit of being honest, but there was such a thing as going too far. "Let's put it this way. I wouldn't have had the nerve to take the job."

He seemed pleased by her admission. "So you approve?"

"You're a good-looking man," she said a little tartly. "I'm sure women have told you that."

"A time or two, yes." His expression went from pleased to smug. "So, what do you want to do today?"

"Work?" Jessica suggested.

He shook his head. "Sounds boring. Let's go sightseeing instead. Franconia Notch, the Flume, the Cannon Mountain Tramway—we're entitled to be tourists once in a while."

It was one of the most confusing days Jessica had ever spent. Any time two people shared one motorcycle there was bound to be intimate contact, and Griff didn't seem to mind at all. On the contrary, he was solicitous, charming and amusing, almost as if he were courting her. What baffled her was that he did none of the things a man might do to show a romantic interest in a woman. He never even touched her, much less kissed her. By the time they got back to the campground she had no idea what to think. She only knew that she was frustrated and unsettled. More and more, she wanted Griff to hold her—to kiss her as he'd kissed her on Grand Isle.

They were looking at the campground bulletin board to find out what the nightly movie was when somebody called Jessica's name. She ignored it, thinking the man must want some other Jessica, but then he called to her again. "Hey, Jessie Lynn! What are *you* doing up here? Did you run off with the dude in the awesome pants?"

She turned around. Only one person called her Jessie Lynn—her cousin Todd. Sure enough, he was standing there with one of his fraternity brothers from Dartmouth, a boy one year older who'd always struck Jessica as a little too streetwise for his own good.

"I'm working," she answered. "This is Dr. Arthur Marshall, a sociology professor at Harvard. I'm assisting him with a study he's conducting. Dr. Marshall, this is my cousin Todd and his friend Sonny.''

Griff had a preoccupied look on his face as he shook their hands. "It's nice to meet you. I should get back to the trailer and do some work." He reached into his pocket, removed his wallet, and handed Jessica a single dollar. "Why don't you stop at the store and pick up some extra food? Your cousin and his friend can join us for dinner."

Jessica and the two boys stood there in silence until he'd disappeared from view. Then Todd said, "I don't believe those clothes or that haircut. And does the guy think inflation stopped in 1950?"

"He's a little eccentric," Jessica said distractedly. He'd also put on quite a performance—the same sort of performance, she realized, as he'd once put on for her. Who *was* Griff Marshall, anyway? Surely not the preoccupied, absentminded man who'd just wandered off down the road. "He's not a bad guy to work for," she added. "How about you? What are you doing here?"

"Fishing, mostly. We got in yesterday." Todd grinned at her. "Small world, huh?"

"Did Alex tell you I was here?" Jessica couldn't imagine his betraying a confidence that way, but no other explanation came to mind.

Todd frowned. "Alex? Haven't seen him in weeks."

"Mrs. MacPherson—"

"Haven't seen her, either. We were over at school, visiting some of the guys, and we decided to drive to the mountains for some fishing and hiking." The three of them started toward the general store. "The rest of the family might be looking for you, but not me. If you want to stay hidden, that's fine with me."

Knowing Todd as she did, Jessica believed it. He wasn't the type to concern himself with something so serious as the sale of the family company.

She picked up some chicken and soft drinks and told Todd she'd expect him and Sonny in an hour. Griff was in his room when she returned, either working or sleeping, so she got dinner in the oven as quietly as she could. They hadn't conducted any real interviews that day but they'd chatted casually with quite a few people. She figured she might as well make a few notes.

Todd was his usual ebullient self that evening, telling stories that might or might not have been true but were certainly very funny. More than a few of them were at the expense of his friends, including Sonny, who finally said kiddingly, "You'd better watch your step, pal. The Petronelli clan doesn't appreciate people making fun of us."

Todd held up his hands in mock terror. "I'm sorry, I'm sorry. I'll stick to my own family from now on. I've got more stories about them than I could tell in a month." He winked at Jessica. "They deserve having people make fun of them, don't you think? They're the craziest bunch of fruitcakes east of California."

"If you mean their quarrel about the shoe company—"

"What else? Ernest runs around threatening to commit suicide unless he keeps control and my father runs around threatening to murder Ernest unless the opposite happens. Either way, it doesn't look good for Ernest." He paused. "So what are you going to do? Hide out in the mountains till the fifteenth?"

"Exactly," Jessica said. She wasn't about to confide her real itinerary, not when his father would wheedle it out of him and show up in Maine to press his case.

Griff had been silent all evening, playing the preoccupied professor again, but Jessica didn't doubt he'd listened intently. He was no more absentminded than she was. Now he looked at Todd and said mildly, "You behave as if you had no stake in the decision that will eventually be made. Surely you have an opinion as to whether or not the sale should go through."

Todd shrugged. "Not much of one, Dr. Marshall. Oh, sure, I sympathize with my father—after all, he's my father. The guy has worked like a dog all these years to make the company successful, but the truth is that he could have done better financially by selling his share of the firm and reinvesting in income-producing securities. Ernest doesn't have the cash to buy Dad out and he would need a three-fourths vote of the board to sell his stock to an outsider. Since Ernest would never agree to that, Dad is stuck at Lawrence Shoes. All he knows are shoes. He hates shoes. He has the soul of a painter but he's stuck with shoes. I wish he could do what he really wants."

"Indeed. His reasons for wanting to sell are compelling, but your Uncle Ernest's reasons for wanting to do the opposite are equally so. It's a dilemma, Mr. Lawrence, a moral and philosophical conundrum." Griff stood up. "If you'll excuse me, I have to make a phone call. I'm sure I'll see you when I return." He gave a polite nod of his head and walked out the door.

"Geez, that guy is strange," Todd said once Griff was out of earshot. "You're sure you're okay staying with him?"

Jessica got up to clear away the dishes. "You know professors. They live in their own private worlds."

Todd and Sonny continued to talk and joke as she cleaned up the kitchen. She listened with half an ear, thinking about Griff. He wasn't an oddball at all, merely a human chameleon who could do everything from fight like Rambo to spew out computer jargon like a Silicon Valley genius. What secrets was he keeping? What was he hiding in that locked nightstand of his?

A few minutes later she set a plate of brownies on the table and regarded Todd thoughtfully. He was charming and entertaining, but certainly no angel. Sometimes she wondered if he hadn't gotten into a lot more trouble than Charles had ever admitted.

"Dr. Marshall *can* be mysterious," she said nonchalantly. "In fact, he keeps his nightstand locked all the time. I've always wondered what he thinks is so important." She gave Todd an ingenuous look. "Do you suppose you could pick the lock?"

He took a knife out of his pocket, the kind that had every little gadget ever invented attached to its base. "I could try, but somebody better stand guard. Sonny?"

"Sure. Call me if you run into a problem." His tone implied that Todd was a rank amateur compared to him.

The locks proved surprisingly strong, but Todd finally got them open with a wickedly pointed little instrument that was sharp enough to turn a metal bowl into a colander. They jimmied the door on the bottom first, finding pretty much what Jessica had expected—books, reports and journals. She'd seen some of them on Griff's bed when he was working and assumed they were references for his lectures. There was also a stack of yellow legal pads, but all of them were filled with notes. Jessica couldn't imagine how he'd accomplished so much in only two weeks.

Todd relocked the nightstand door and went to work on the drawer. He gave a low whistle when he finally got it open. "Now that's a fancy-looking little item. I wouldn't have thought he was the type to own it."

The "item" was a large gun, and just looking at it made Jessica shudder. The closest she'd come to violence was when she'd watched Griff fight O'Reilly. "Marshall knows judo," she said. "I know it's hard to picture, but last week I saw him take on a guy—"

She was cut off by a low but urgent warning from Sonny. "Hurry it up, folks. I just spotted him down the road."

Todd hurriedly closed the drawer, inserted the ice pick instrument in the keyhole, and worked it around until the lock mechanism clicked into place. By the time Griff opened the door the three of them were sitting at the table talking.

Jessica felt guilty about snooping and was afraid it showed. Still, she was curious about the notes and gun. There hadn't been a single blank pad in that nightstand, so what did he do at night? And why did he carry a gun? O'Reilly to the contrary, distinguished sociology professors weren't supposed to find themselves in situations where they'd need one.

Todd and Sonny stayed the rest of the evening, telling Jessica about their plans for the rest of the summer and asking Griff about his work. As they were getting ready to leave, Todd apologetically mentioned that he would have to tell his father he'd seen her. "I know you don't want to be found, but he's been worried about you, Jessie. He'll want to know you're okay."

"I sent him a postcard from Lake George," Jessica said. "He knows I'm working out of town and that I'm fine."

"He'd still like to speak to you—"

"I thought you didn't care one way or the other," Griff interrupted.

"I don't, but Dad does." Todd gave Jessica a pleading look. "He's an artist, just like you. Are shoes really so important in this world? I mean, who cares about whether Lawrence oxfords come with a two-year guarantee? One beautiful painting is worth a thousand Lawrence oxfords."

Not to you, Jessica thought, *so why the heartrending plea?* "I've tried to explain," she said aloud. "I don't want to get caught in the middle."

A trace of impatience entered his voice. "Be reasonable, Jessica. If Grandma and Grandpa had been opposed to selling they would have put something in their wills to prevent it. It isn't as if either of them died unexpectedly."

In Jessica's opinion, they hadn't put anything in their wills because it had never occurred to them that either of their sons would consider selling. "I don't think that matters at this point. I just want to stay out of it."

"But you must have an opinion. Both of us know that my parents have done a lot more for you than Ernest and Rita ever did. Your music—where would you be if they hadn't taken your side?"

"Todd, that's not fair—"

"Why not? You're not going to make a career out of selling shoes any more than I am!" Todd was openly exasperated now. "How else are you supposed to make a decision, if not by who you owe the most to?"

"By who's right!" Jessica snapped. She'd never yelled at Todd in her life but found his lectures offensive. He was two years younger than she, totally irresponsible, and didn't know what it meant to be torn by conflicting loyalties.

Even so, she was surprised by what came out next. "Don't you understand? I agree with Ernest! I was raised by Grandma and Grandpa from the time I was eight and I believe all those things about quality and loyalty to your customers. At the same time, I'm more grateful to your father and mother than somebody as selfish as you are can probably imagine. The best favor I can do for them is to stay out of it completely, because if you drag me back to Boston and force me to vote..." She let the sentence hang. Todd had whitened, so obviously he understood what a mistake he'd just made.

She was only half-aware that Griff had come over to stand beside her. "We'll see you tomorrow," he said to Todd. Todd must have caught the hint of command in his voice, because he didn't argue. Muttering an apology to Jessica, he said a hasty good night and followed Sonny out of the camper.

Jessica was so distraught she was shaking. She hated scenes. Despite all Todd's faults, she loved him and was upset that she'd yelled at him. Most of all, she was shaken by the admission she'd made—not only to Todd, but to herself. She'd had no idea that she sided with Ernest so strongly.

"Maybe I should stop running away," she said to Griff. "Maybe I should go back to Boston and vote my convictions."

"And alienate half your family? There are other stockholders, Jessica. Let your uncles fight for *their* hearts and minds." He took her into his arms and gently pulled her closer until her head was resting against his chest. "Even if the sale goes through, Ernest would always have the option of buying back the company if things don't work out. It happens all the time with deals like this."

Jessica felt a little of the tension leave her body. "Do you really think so?"

"I know so. I wouldn't be surprised if it's already in the contract." He started to rub her back, rhythmically and soothingly. Sighing heavily, she closed her eyes and snuggled against his chest. She couldn't remember feeling so safe, not ever in her life.

Chapter Ten

For once, Griff told himself the following morning, he'd handled Jessica exactly right. He'd calmed her down and eased her fears, then pecked her good night on the forehead in a way that could have been either platonic or romantic, depending on how she chose to interpret it. The kiss had been a compromise—a means of hinting at his feelings without frightening her back to Boston. Every time he thought about her hornet's nest of a family there, he became more determined than ever to keep her at his side.

Only the day before, Roxy had given him some additional information—on Todd Lawrence, of all people. Todd's scrapes hadn't been just minor. They included getting a girlfriend pregnant, nearly flunking out of school and being arrested for grand theft auto—he'd hot-wired an expensive sports car and taken a joyride around Boston. His father kept getting him off the hook, but Roxy had talked to an elderly friend of Jessica's grandparents who knew about the grief Todd had caused them and had irately repeated everything. Charles was at the end of his tether, the woman said, and had threatened to cut the boy off without a penny if he got into any more trouble.

Now an even more disturbing element had entered the picture in the person of Todd's friend Sonny. The minute Griff had heard the name Petronelli, he'd wondered if Sonny could be any relation to Frank Petronelli, a high-level thug he'd run across during his FBI days. The boy's reference to "the clan" had made Griff even more uneasy, so he'd called up Roxy and asked her to check it out. If Todd was running around with one of Frank's relatives, there was more reason than ever to keep Jessica away from Boston. The Frank Petronellis of this world had ways of applying very persuasive pressure on people.

Griff didn't believe for a moment that Todd's appearance in New Hampshire had been coincidental. Ulanoff had to have told him where to go, but why, Griff didn't know. At best, Ulanoff might have seen Todd as harmless and thought Jessica would enjoy a visit from him, and at worst, he might have an agenda of his own. According to Jessica, Ulanoff had given her the same advice as Griff had—to stay out of the family quarrel—but Griff didn't trust the man. According to Roxy, he cheated and gambled compulsively. He'd also paid a hefty sum to get Jessica out of town. If loving concern was his motive, why was he running around with other women?

Griff was so suspicious of the people around Jessica that he'd even asked Roxy to check out Mrs. MacPherson. She was supposed to be visiting her daughter in Seattle, but for all he knew, she could be running a floating crap game out of Jessica's Beacon Hill home. One way or another, he meant to keep Jessica out of reach, even though it would mean changing their travel plans.

Half an hour later he walked out of his room wearing orange pants and a brown polyester shirt decorated with orange brush marks and Degas ballerinas. Jessica was sitting at the table, reading some kind of letter. Griff took one look at her tousled hair and crimson robe and swallowed hard. This business of traveling together was getting tougher all the time.

She said a husky good morning and handed him the letter. It was from Todd, who wrote that he and Sonny had decided to return to Hanover. "I found this stuck in the door when I went outside to check the temperature," she said. "It's going to be a scorcher today."

Griff's guard went up. He had no way of knowing if Todd had actually left. Suppose he came around while Jessica was alone and threatened her? "I have to go into town today to buy some presents for my nieces," he said. "Could you help me pick them out?"

She seemed pleased to be asked. "I'll go get dressed."

"It's only eight-thirty. Take your time." Griff resisted the urge to grab her and kiss her good morning as she passed him on the way to the bathroom.

The urge got stronger when she reappeared in the galley. Her shorts and tank top were sexy enough to dissolve the best of good intentions. He somehow kept them in place as they browsed through the local shops, but when they came to a barber, the lovesick male in him took over. He wanted Jessica to find him attractive.

He gestured toward the shop door. "Would you mind? I never seem to get around to this at home."

She gave a throaty laugh. "Really? I never noticed!"

Much to his satisfaction, she was staring rather than laughing by the time he got out of the chair. "So what do you think?" he asked, already knowing the answer. She liked what she saw. If she liked it enough, maybe she would lose a few of her inhibitions and make the first move.

He spent the rest of the day doing his damnedest to bring that about, but nothing worked. He took her swimming in the campground lake and rubbed lotion all over her back, deliberating trying to arouse her. He fed her a delicious dinner and cleaned up afterward, doing his best to spoil her. He asked her to play the flute for him and sat on the couch listening, all but devouring her with his eyes. Tactics like that had gotten him invited into more than one woman's apartment, but Jessica ignored them. The looks she gave him when she thought he wasn't watching told him she was only pretending not to respond, but she was either too shy or too proper to admit how she felt and do something about it.

After two hours of playing she set down her flute and smiled uncertainly. "The soloist has to stop. She's about to fall asleep."

"The soloist was wonderful," Griff said. "Someday she's going to make her debut with the Boston Symphony, and I'll be in the audience watching."

She started to pack away her flute. "You'll have to sit upstairs with a pair of opera glasses if you want to see me. The flutes are in back."

"Who's talking about the orchestra?" Griff teased. "I meant when you appear as a soloist."

Jessica laughed and said her ambitions didn't extend that far, but Griff could see she was flattered. Their eyes met and held. The expression on her face was so evocative his body tautened in anticipation. He'd never seen such a mixture of desire, wariness and confusion.

He told himself to wait, that she would eventually offer what he wanted, but he was so aroused that patience was simply beyond him. He held out his hand. "Come over here a minute."

Jessica hesitated, then started forward. She was still clutching her flute case when she stopped in front of his knees.

He reached up, grasped her by the hips and eased her onto his lap. She didn't resist, but she didn't look at him, either. Tucking a finger under her chin, he turned her face toward his. "I want to kiss you," he said softly.

Her eyes dropped. "I don't think that would be a good idea."

"No?" Griff smiled. "I think it's a terrific idea."

"But we hardly know each other. Or at least, I hardly know you. You never talk about yourself."

"I'm single, I'm respectably employed, and I promise not to seduce you." He put his arms around her and drew her closer. She stiffened but didn't pull away. When their lips were only inches apart, he added as persuasively as he could, "We matter to each other, Jessica. What else do you need to know?"

She was breathing rapidly and her pupils were dilated with excitement. If ever a woman wanted to be kissed, Jessica did, but what she said was, "Please, Griff. Let me go."

Acceding to her wishes was one of the toughest things Griff had ever done. He was sure she wanted him to override her objections and kiss away her doubts, but he didn't dare. Suppose she had second thoughts? Suppose she decided she was in over her head, and ran back to Boston and alleged safety? He was convinced Boston was anything *but* safe.

It was only much later, when his desire had cooled and he was lying alone in bed, that a quiet sense of satisfaction set in. She'd been relieved when he released her, but she'd also been disappointed. Frustration was eating at her almost as badly as it was eating at him. When she finally cracked, the explosion was going to rival Mount St. Helens.

Why did I stop him? Jessica asked herself that question over and over, but was no closer to an answer in the morning than she'd been the previous night.

Was it the mysteries surrounding Griff, the conflicting impressions he'd given her? Was it her unresolved relationship with Alex? Was it simple panic, or even a cowardly refusal to admit she wanted him, and take responsibility for the consequences? She didn't know.

Maybe, she thought during breakfast that morning, it had something to do with his looks. She gave him a surreptitious glance as he picked up his coffee. He was more handsome than ever now that he'd gotten a decent haircut. Oddly enough, he was less gray, too. And when he'd taken off his shirt at the lake—when he'd massaged suntan lotion into her back so languorously and erotically... She sighed and took a bite of toast. She didn't want to think about how many women he must have made love to. Griff was probably as experienced as he was attractive, and maybe that was the problem. She didn't want to be the latest conquest on his list.

She was afraid he might be angry with her, but he continued to shower her with charm and indulgence. He even seemed quietly amused, perhaps by her naïveté, perhaps by her ambivalence. It was as if he were sure he would win in the end.

Since they were leaving that morning, she started tidying the camper as soon as they finished eating. She was putting away the last of the dishes when Griff came back from disconnecting the hookups. "There seemed to be a leak in one of the lines," he said, "so I went down to the office and called my cousin in Scarborough. She knows a place that can fix it, but in the meantime, she invited us to stay at her house."

Jessica was about to make the usual polite protests when she realized he was handing her a golden opportunity. Maybe this cousin of his could tell her more about him. "As long as it's no trouble," she said. "I could always stay in a motel."

"Their kids are at camp right now. Janet said you could use their room."

Jessica nodded and followed him to the front of the camper. As he pulled out of their site, he told her that his cousin was a high school history teacher married to a physician. "William is always working, so Janet loves having company around. She'll probably drag us all over town, showing us historic buildings." He grinned at her. "I suppose the tourists at Henry Wadsworth Longfellow's house will be just as interesting to interview as the ones at beaches and parks."

"It could add a whole new dimension to your study," Jessica teased. "You'll get the *Masterpiece Theatre* crowd in addition to the recreation nuts."

Her words proved more prophetic than she could have imagined. She'd assumed they'd only be staying with Griff's cousin for a day or two, but the camper needed more extensive repairs than they'd expected and there was a problem about getting the parts. In the meantime, Janet took them to museums and art galleries, restored mansions and old lighthouses, on a walking tour of the seaport district and on on a cruise of Portland harbor.

Griff struck up conversations everywhere they went. There were so many of those brief interviews that Jessica's head was reeling at the end of each day. It was all she could do to get something down on paper, much less be sure her notes were complete and accurate.

She never got a chance to talk to Janet about Griff because they were never alone long enough for personal conversations. As for Griff himself, she was never alone with him at all. They weren't even on the same floor—the guest room was behind the living room while the girls' room was upstairs.

Even with the physical separation, he managed to keep her off balance. He would take her arm to politely help her over bumpy or slick terrain and her skin would begin to tingle. He would touch her face to draw her attention to something in a museum and her heart would start to hammer. He didn't have to take her in his arms to arouse her—all he had to do was smile or tease her.

She was falling in love with him, and the sensation was both frightening and intoxicating. How could she love him when she knew so little about him? She was so intent on trying to figure him out that it took her days to come up with the most obvious solution of all. Arthur G. Marshall was a famous sociologist. Any decent college library would contain information about him. The use of such libraries was usually restricted to students and other school personnel, but she had a good friend who taught not fifty miles away at Pierce University in Portsmouth, New Hampshire.

She raised the subject at dinner Thursday night, after Janet had outlined her plans to take them to Kennebunkport the following day. "Would you mind if I didn't go? I've got a friend in Portsmouth who I haven't seen in nearly a year and I'd like to visit her. I could take a bus."

"Don't be silly," Janet said. "Portsmouth's not that much farther than Kennebunkport. I'll run you down there." She looked at Griff. "Is that okay?"

Griff shrugged and said it was fine. As soon as dinner was over, Jessica called her friend Gail, got directions to her apartment, and arranged to meet her at eleven o'clock. It had been so ludicrously easy that she could have kicked herself for not thinking of it sooner.

Gail was watching from the window when Griff dropped Jessica off the next morning. The first words out of her mouth as she opened the door weren't "Hi, Jessica," or "It's great to see you," but "Who was the hunk?"

"A professor named Arthur Marshall. Have you heard of him?"

"I took four sociology courses in college," Gail answered. "Of course I've heard of him, but that can't be Arthur Marshall. He's much too young."

"That's what I thought at first, but he interviewed me in his office, I've seen him sign travelers' checks, and I heard someone call him by name." Jessica explained about the job she'd taken and the suspicions she'd gradually developed. "Do you think we could stop by the library?" she asked. "I want to look him up in the catalog."

Fifteen minutes later Gail was seated at a computer terminal in the main reference room while Jessica watched over her shoulder. Gail typed out Marshall, Arthur G., and a long list of books came up on the screen. The earliest title had been published over thirty years before. "Precocious little devil, wasn't he?" Gail drawled.

"Very. Whoever he really is, I'd like to wring his neck." Actually, Jessica had a very good idea of who he was. She even knew how to check it out. "Gail, do they have any out-of-state phone books in this library?"

Gail pointed to her left. "Over by the wall."

They found a listing for an Arthur G. Marshall, Sr. in Cambridge. Even though Marshall didn't use Sr. on his books and Griff hadn't used Jr. on his travelers' checks, Jessica was sure it was a case of father and son. She jotted down Marshall's number and returned to Gail's apartment to make the call.

She asked the woman who answered the phone if Dr. Marshall were in, and was told he was in his office at Harvard. "You could try him there if you like," the woman suggested.

"Perhaps there's some mistake," Jessica said, knowing darn well there wasn't. "If this is Mrs. Marshall—I mean, Griff didn't tell me he was married."

The woman laughed. "He's not. This is his mother. Actually, he's on vacation right now."

"Oh. Well, do you know how I could reach him, Mrs. Marshall? I'd really like to get in touch with him—or even just leave him a message somewhere."

Mrs. Marshall sighed. "I wish I could help you, dear, but Griff...he'll call you if he wants to see you. I'm sorry."

It was all Jessica could do not to slam down the phone. In the first place, the miserable, womanizing scoundrel had so many women chasing after him he'd forbidden his mother to give out his unlisted number. And in the second, what was he doing running around impersonating his father? Neck-wringing wasn't good enough for him, but she was at a loss to say what *was*.

She could barely control her temper when he and Janet arrived to pick her up. Jessica was too well-mannered to cause a scene in front of Janet, but the moment she got Griff alone she was going to lace into him like a shark into a guppy. She gave him the dirtiest look she could muster as he helped her into the car, but it rolled right off his back. He simply grinned and continued his conversation with Janet.

Much to Jessica's surprise, the camper was in the driveway when they got back. They went inside to investigate and found a note from the mechanic who'd driven it over, along with Griff's copy of a presigned credit card slip. Jessica was about to suggest that she and Griff remain inside to talk when Janet started coaxing him to leave. "I'm absolutely starved," she said. "William swore he'd be home early, so the kitchen is all yours." She looked at Jessica. "Griff is doing the cooking tonight. He's making sweet and sour chicken."

The next few hours were some of the longest of Jessica's life. She was furious with Griff; not only had he lied about who he was, he didn't seem to care that he'd upset her. It was almost as if he knew what she'd discovered in Portsmouth but didn't consider it important.

She volunteered to clean up after dinner, knowing she needed some time alone to settle herself down and plan what she would say. When the last pot was washed and the last counter wiped, she walked into the living room where Griff was talking to Janet and William and gave him a sweet smile. "Griff? Could I speak to you privately for a minute?"

"Sure. Go ahead to the camper. I'll be out in a moment."

Jessica paced around like a caged lioness as "a moment" stretched into five minutes. As soon as Griff walked in, she said the words she'd been rehearsing for the past half hour. Every syllable dripped sarcasm.

"You really are amazing, Dr. Marshall. After all, your first book was published thirty-three years ago. Tell me, did you research it while you were in preschool?"

He never batted an eyelash. "Actually, I wasn't born yet when *Extended Families in Post-War America* came out. I was thirty last March."

Her hands clenched into fists at her sides. "How can you stand there so calmly? Don't you realize I'd like to kill you? You lied to me—the way you looked—the stubble and the haircut—the baggy clothing—the absentminded professor routine..." She was sputtering with rage. "And those stupid glasses! I'll bet you don't even need them."

He took them off and set them on the counter. "Right."

"Your wardrobe—those hideous clothes . . ."

"You don't like my clothes?"

He sounded so forlorn that Jessica was sure she'd hurt his feelings. She might have been livid, but nastiness was foreign to her nature. She was about to apologize when he burst out laughing, making her more cross than ever. "The only thing worse than your clothing is *you*!" she snapped. "You're nothing but a—a lying, conniving, superficial, womanizing *skunk*!"

"Womanizing?" he repeated, looking wounded.

"Don't you dare deny it! I spoke to your mother. You've got so many women after you, you won't even let her give out your phone number. Your *unlisted* phone number, I might add. Is that how you keep them out of your hair once you've dumped them? By refusing to tell them how to get hold of you?"

He stood there with his arms folded across his chest, not saying a word. "Well?" Jessica finally demanded. "Aren't you going to answer me?"

"You'll have to calm down first. I don't cope well with hysterical women." He gave her a lazy smile. "Even when they're beautiful and passionate."

Jessica raised her chin a fraction. "I can't imagine why! You've probably had lots of experience in that department—not that I'm any of the things you mentioned."

"You sound pretty hysterical to me," he observed.

"I am not hysterical," Jessica insisted. "I just want some answers."

"Not beautiful, either?" He shook his head. "I'm sorry, but I'll have to disagree."

"Save your lines for women who take them seriously. I told you—"

"And not passionate? No way. That's something I know about firsthand, and believe me, you're *extremely* passionate. But go on. You were saying?"

Jessica wasn't saying anything because she was too stunned to talk. He could only be referring to one thing—that night in his room. "You knew who I was," she finally choked out.

"Of course I did. You were delightful." He walked over and took her arm. "You look a bit faint, darling. Can I get you a glass of water?"

Jessica shrugged away his hand. "No, and don't you dare *darling* me. I'm fine." All the same, she went over to the sofa and sat down. This interview wasn't going the way she'd expected. Beautiful? Passionate? Delightful? Did he really think so?

Griff joined her on the sofa, sitting a little too close for her peace of mind. "If you want to blame anyone," he said, "blame your friend Ulanoff. It all started when my father happened to mention that I'd agreed to do some research for him this summer. Dad didn't have the time—let's face it, it *is* a fairly offbeat topic for the great Arthur G. Marshall— and he knew I planned to go camping, so he asked me to do some interviewing. I was glad to help, except that writing isn't my strong point. I'm a computer consultant. Dad told Alex I was looking for someone to listen to the interviews and write them up, which was all Alex had to hear. He wanted you out of town, but he was sure you'd never agree to take the job if you knew he'd arranged it."

"So he asked you to put an ad in the paper." Jessica hadn't forgotten that Alex was the one who'd brought the ad to her attention in the first place. She wasn't so much angry now as humiliated. "I suppose I was the only one you even interviewed," she said.

Griff smiled at her. "My father and Alex are friends. I didn't mind doing Alex a favor and taking you along. From what he told me, I figured you for the repressed virgin type, which of course turned out to be only half-correct—"

"I don't think that's funny," Jessica said stiffly.

"Just stating the facts, ma'am. Anyway, you obviously wouldn't have come with me if you'd known I was a thirty-year-old Adonis, so I, uh, altered my appearance a little so I could pass myself off as my father and soft-pedaled my incredible charm."

Thirty-year-old Adonis? Womanizing egomaniac was more like it! "Conceited Don Juan," Jessica said aloud.

"It was a joke, Jessica." He touched her shoulder to get her attention. "Give me a break, honey. I'm not such a bad guy. There haven't been that many women in my life—the reason my mother doesn't give out my phone number is that she knows I have a hang-up about privacy." He paused a moment. "Look, you walked into my Dad's office weighing a hundred pounds soaking wet and acting scared of your own shadow. How was I supposed to know you'd turn out to be beautiful, hypersensitive and—"

"Hypersensitive? You have the nerve to call me hypersensitive? You were the rudest, coldest, most condescending—"

"I was trying to keep you in line. You're too damn curious and quick-witted for your own good. I didn't know how to handle you." He touched her shoulder again, but this time he left his hand there. "You're turning me inside out, Jessica. I'm sorry about lying to you, but once it got started I didn't know how to stop it. I was afraid you'd get mad and refuse to see me again if you found out I wasn't my father."

Jessica's hands were clenched together in her lap, twisting and intertwining. How much of this could she believe?

Obviously he was Arthur Marshall's son, and obviously the initiative for the whole charade had come from Alex, but what about the rest of it? Did he care for her as much as he seemed to?

Memories came flooding back. That night in his room he hadn't tried to take advantage of her, although he easily could have. The evening Todd had upset her so badly, he'd held and comforted her. He hadn't made a pass. And the other night in the camper, he'd let her go the moment she'd asked him to. Those were hardly the actions of a Don Juan.

"Who's Roxy?" she finally asked.

"Somebody I work with. It was the first name I could think of that night. Things were getting out of hand, and I was trying to find a way to cut them off without, uh—"

"Embarrassing me?" Jessica suggested. "Having me run home to Boston?"

"Something like that, yes."

She took a deep breath. "You promise you're really a computer consultant?"

"Yes."

She'd heard enough incomprehensible jargon come out of his mouth to believe it, but that still didn't explain the judo and the gun. "For a computer scientist, you defend yourself very well," she said.

He moved a little closer and put his arm around her shoulders. Jessica had the feeling he was moving in for the kill, but didn't pull away. She wasn't angry anymore, just confused—about him and about her own feelings.

"I was a computer expert for the FBI for four years before I went into business for myself," he said. "I had all the standard training."

A former FBI agent? Jessica could hardly take it in. "I suppose that explains the gun," she murmured to herself. He must be used to carrying one.

It was the first time all evening she'd caught him off guard, and the irony of it was that she hadn't even meant to. "You picked the locks?" he asked incredulously.

"Todd did," she answered.

"It figures." He gave a disgusted shake of his head. "So tell me, Jessica, what else have I botched? What else do you know that I don't know you know?"

Jessica finally felt like something other than a fool. A former FBI agent, and she'd actually outwitted him! There was something supremely satisfying about that. "Well, I happened to overhear that phone call to Roxy in Lake George, when you asked her to check out Alex and my relatives. Did you and Roxy work together at the Bureau, too?"

He looked positively grim. "No, but I've kept up with my old colleagues. She knew who to call for information."

"And what did she find out?"

"I'd rather not say."

Jessica could think of only one reason for that. He was trying to shield her from some unpleasant truths. "That bad, huh?" she said.

He didn't answer.

His silence told her how silly she was being. He might have lied to her about who he was, but in every other way he'd been as gentle, honorable and protective as a woman could wish. Alex and her relatives seemed totally unimportant at that moment.

She fingered his top button, then pushed it through the buttonhole. As far as she was concerned, the serious part of the interrogation was over. "I'm waiting," she said in a sultry voice. "What did she find out?"

Griff stared at her hand, which was working its way down his shirt. "Uh, Jessica—"

"This shirt is hideous. I don't see why I should have to look at it." She ran her finger lightly over his chest. The knife scars were only faintly visible now, but they still made her shudder in remembered fear. "I want information, Mr. Marshall. Or is it Dr. Marshall?"

"Mr." His voice was low and hoarse. "Look, Jessica, you don't love Alex. I know you don't or you wouldn't be touching me this way. And your uncles..."

"Yes?" She was caressing his nipple now, enjoying the helpless hunger in his eyes.

"How do you expect me to talk when you keep doing that?" he groaned.

"I thought FBI agents had to learn to withstand torture."

"That's the CIA." He pulled her into his arms, buried his hand in her hair, and brought her lips to his mouth.

Jessica turned away at the last possible moment. "Oh, no, you don't," she said, laughing. "Not until you answer my questions."

"You know what happens to women who tease?" He pushed against her shoulders until she tumbled onto her back. "They get teased right back."

Within moments he'd covered her body with his own. The intimate contact was so electrifying that questions and answers went straight from her head. "Teased how?" she whispered.

He nuzzled her neck. "You'll see. When you're ready to give up, just say so. Who knows? Maybe you'll get what you want." His teeth found her lips and playfully nipped them. Jessica shivered and closed her eyes. His mouth was warm, knowing and maddeningly elusive. He toyed with her lips until she was so frustrated she grabbed his face in a vain effort to hold him still. Then she probed at his closed mouth with her tongue.

He caught her wrists in his hand and pulled them over her head. "Not yet, lady. I want two things from you first."

Jessica opened her eyes and stared at him, breathing hard. The blasted man looked perfectly calm, not to mention obnoxiously smug. "You don't have to be so pleased with yourself," she grumbled. "What two things?"

"Apologize for teasing me."

She tossed her head. "I will not. You loved every minute of it. You should thank me."

"Okay, then, I'm thanking you. But this—" He grabbed Alex's ring and pulled. "This has to go. I'm sick of seeing it on your finger."

Moments after the ring hit the floor, his tongue found the inside of her mouth and his hand covered her breast. Jessica was so wildly attracted to him that it never occurred to her to hold back. She became a creature of pure, mindless sensation, responding tempestuously to every caress and kiss.

The long, drugging minutes in his arms came to an end when he pulled himself up and jerkily moved away. He ran a shaky hand through his hair. "When you give up, you really give up. I'd like to keep doing this all night, but if we don't get going, we'll miss the ferry."

"The ferry?" Jessica was so light-headed with arousal she was sure she must have misunderstood him.

"To Yarmouth, Nova Scotia. Dad asked me to interview some Canadians for the study. He wants to do some cross-cultural comparisons."

Nova Scotia? Jessica thought. What was he talking about? "I can't go to Nova Scotia with you—not after what just happened."

He stood up and buttoned his shirt. "Nothing happened that hasn't happened to millions of teenagers in millions of backseats in millions of cars. You don't have to worry about packing, by the way. I brought in your things while you were cleaning the kitchen.''

He would have walked up front, but Jessica grabbed him by the fabric of his trousers. "Wait a minute, Griff. You can't drag me off to Canada without us talking this over. You and I—if we stay together—what I'm trying to say is—''

"You won't be able to keep your hands off me?"

She reddened. "I won't be able to say no to you. At least, I'm afraid I won't. And I'm not ready for what you want.''

He caressed her hair, very gently. "Trust me, sweetheart. I wasn't going to ask so soon. I agree that we don't know each other well enough yet. In the meantime, I need somebody to help with Dad's research, and I'll be lonely as hell if it's not you. Please, come with me.''

He was only asking for what Jessica longed to give him. She smiled solemnly, trusting him completely, sure he must be the most perfect man who'd ever walked the earth. Then she nodded in agreement.

Chapter Eleven

Jessica was so totally smitten with Griff that it wasn't until the following morning, when they drove off the ferry in Nova Scotia, that she realized how bewilderingly sudden this trip to Canada was. "When did you talk to your father—about adding to the research, that is?" she asked.

"Yesterday afternoon. I called to tell him how things were going and mentioned that everyone we talked to was beginning to sound alike."

"And he thought Canadians might have a different attitude? Different expectations?"

"He asked me to check into it. Fortunately, there was space on the ferry." He handed her a map of eastern Canada. "Direct me to Greenfield, darling. It's somewhere near Kejimkujik National Park."

Jessica studied the map, basking in the intimacy of his endearments. She felt like a newlywed—beautiful, desirable and blissfully happy. In retrospect, she couldn't imagine why she'd accepted Alex's ring. He was a good friend and she was grateful for all he'd done, but there was more to a good marriage than friendship.

The ring was in her purse now, but she was still troubled by what it symbolized. She was having second thoughts about waiting till she got home to tell Alex she wasn't going to marry him. Maybe it was fairer to do it immediately.

She asked Griff's advice later that afternoon as they strolled through the woods near their campsite. "I hate to string Alex along, but telling him on the phone seems so cold. Still, the least I can do is call him and mention our change in itinerary. He might have tried me in York Harbor and been worried when I wasn't there. If he calls Bar Harbor, too—"

"I don't want you phoning him at all," Griff interrupted.

"But Griff—"

He pulled her into his arms. "Humor me, darling. Don't forget, you were close to marrying him when I met you. Naturally I'm jealous. We'll talk to him together as soon as we get back to Boston."

Like most women in love, Jessica wanted to please the man in her life. Alex hadn't tried to reach her in Grand Isle or North Woodstock so he obviously assumed she was in good hands. Little did he know *how* good, she thought guiltily.

Still, she'd never made him any promises. She hadn't even wanted to accept his ring. Only a masochist would have blamed herself for falling in love with another man, and Jessica was no masochist.

The next couple of days were like a honeymoon. Griff was attentive and affectionate, constantly holding her hand or putting her arm around her and never leaving her on her own. In the evenings, there were long, bone-melting sessions on the sofa that left her weak with pleasure and aching for more. Jessica's grandmother had always warned her that men had about as much self-control as stallions in such situations, but Griff was different. Kissing was as far as it went.

Given the fact that she was walking around on cloud nine most of the time, it wasn't surprising that her usually lively sense of curiosity would temporarily desert her. But even honeymooners had to come down to earth eventually, and reality began to creep in along about Monday.

They'd rented a small boat and were fishing at the time. Griff was wearing a new T-shirt and shorts, neither of which was the slightest bit baggy. Watching him cast, Jessica told herself he looked as much like a computer nerd as Tom Selleck. The thought of his job reminded her that there hadn't even been a business listing under his name in the Boston-area phone books, much less a private listing. How did people who wanted to hire him get in touch with him?

"Tell me about your business," she said. "What's the name of your firm?"

He burst out laughing. "I was wondering when you'd get around to questioning me again. What's the matter? Don't you trust me?"

"Of course I do," she said. "It's just that you still haven't told me much about yourself."

He reeled off a list of his clients, all of them well-known, high-tech companies. "See how respectable I am?"

"But the name of your firm—"

"Is Argo Consultants. The number is 617-555-4321. You want to call and check me out?"

Would he have given her a name and number if he weren't telling the truth? Maybe not, but he *was* an incredibly smooth talker. "If you don't mind, I'll do exactly that," she said.

He gave her an innocent look. "Why should I mind? My life is an open book."

Jessica seriously doubted it, but the receptionist at 617-555-4321 answered the phone with a cheerful, "Good morning, Argo Consultants," and, when Jessica asked for Griff, said he was on vacation. "Would you care to speak with his associate, Ms. Pascal?" she added.

Jessica said no and rang off. Then she asked Griff, "Would Ms. Pascal be your friend, Roxy?"

"Right first time."

"Another computer genius?"

"Almost as good as I am," he said.

She sniffed that his ego was as big as Nova Scotia and took off toward the camper, knowing he would come after her to exact revenge. Everything should have been perfect after that, but niggling little inconsistencies kept eating at her. Why hadn't his mother given her his business number when she'd mentioned leaving a message? Why had he waited until the last possible moment to tell her they were going to Canada? And why was he so dead set against her calling Alex? She couldn't get past the feeling he was still hiding something from her.

She was practicing the flute that same afternoon when an odd snippet of information, long forgotten, suddenly came to mind. Her cousin Emily had had a friend in school who was always bragging about her older sister—how she'd taken a job as a secretary to a private investigator after her divorce, done so well she was now the man's partner, and was always having intriguing, thrilling adventures. Jessica couldn't remember either sister's name, but Emily surely would. Maybe this private investigator could prepare a report on Griff.

The only problem with her plan was that Griff hadn't let her out of his sight since Friday. At that very moment, he

was sitting on the sofa while she practiced. Her eyes lit on
the book of exercises at her feet. Given how he felt about
scales and exercises, she doubted he would stick around
once she began to practice them.

He lasted all of ten minutes. As soon as he'd fled to his
room, Jessica took out her tape recorder, pushed the *re-
cord* button and resumed her playing. Half an hour later she
rewound the tape, set the machine to play back what she'd
just recorded, and slipped out of the camper.

She ran all the way to the campground store and shut
herself into a phone booth. Emily, thank heavens, was
home, and was very surprised to hear from her.

She was even more surprised when Jessica told her what
she wanted. "Talk about coincidences," she said with a
laugh. "When you first disappeared, I had exactly the same
idea. I even called Francie for her sister's number, but her
sister was too busy to take the case. At that point I decided
to forget the whole thing. I couldn't really blame you for
wanting to stay out of it—both Dad and Uncle Charles are
acting like jerks." She paused. "Jessica, Ron and I still want
you to be my maid of honor, even if you vote the other way.
You do realize that, don't you?"

Jessica's throat got tight. "If you want the truth, I'm on
your side, but it's just so difficult. My music—"

"I know. Uncle Charles was there for you but Mom and
Dad weren't. Don't worry about it, okay? Listen, about
Francie's sister—her name is Roxy Pascal and she works for
Argo Investigations in Boston. I even remember the num-
ber. It's 555-4321."

If Jessica hadn't been sitting down she would have wound
up on the floor. She was silent for such a long time that
Emily finally prompted, "Jessica? Are you still there?"

"Yes." She was almost too shell-shocked to speak. "Emily—Roxy isn't—she's not some kind of—of computer whiz, is she?"

"Computer whiz?" Emily repeated. "I doubt it. I mean, she was only a secretary at first, so how could she be?"

The answer was that she couldn't. She was a private investigator, just as Griff was, and neither of them probably knew two bits about computers. My God, what was she even doing with him? What did he want from her?

She thanked Emily for her help and slowly stood up. There was no need to call Argo now. She didn't have the slightest doubt that Argo Investigations was the firm's actual name, that Griff was in charge, and that he'd instructed his receptionist to answer Argo Consultants just in case Jessica called to check on his story.

She opened the door and mechanically walked out. She felt numb all over, unable to grasp what was happening to her. All these people—Alex, Griff's father and Griff; Griff and Roxy; Roxy and Emily—they all seemed to be connected. Where did she fit in?

She hadn't taken more than a few steps when somebody touched her shoulder, startling her so badly she jumped and cried out. She jerked around, saw Griff standing there, and warily backed away.

He smiled at her. "The old tape recorder trick only works on TV."

So he'd followed her. He knew exactly whom she called and exactly what she'd learned. She turned on her heel and walked away. It was beside the point that she had no place to run to.

He hurried after her. "Jessica, listen to me. Everything I did, I did to protect you. There's a lot you don't know—"

"Because you either lied to me or refused to answer my questions," she said.

"I didn't lie to you—not about anything important."

The statement was enough to stop her in her tracks. "Oh, really? Then you're actually doing sociological research?"

"No, but—"

"But nothing. Leave me alone."

She picked up her pace, but he matched her step for step. "Listen to me, damn it! Alex hired me. He knew my father from Harvard and he'd heard I was a private investigator. Most of my work *is* computer-related—"

"Do you honestly expect me to believe that?" Jessica asked. "Or anything else you say?"

"What am I supposed to do? Find the nearest main-frame and reprogram it? Damn it, slow down a little!" He sighed in exasperation. "I have a master's degree from M.I.T. I spent four years with the FBI. Most of my cases deal with industrial espionage or computer fraud, but I do my share of run-of-the-mill stakeouts, too. I was about to go on vacation when Alex called. He told me he wanted you out of Boston—that your uncles were driving you crazy. *He's* the playwright, Jessica, not me. Do you honestly think *I* could come up with such a crazy cover story?"

Given how glib he was, Jessica didn't doubt it. "I suppose you took the case out of the goodness of your heart," she said acidly.

"That and twenty-five hundred a week. It sounded like a paid vacation." He paused, then added softly, "I didn't count on falling in love with you."

Love! Jessica thought in disgust. What a bull artist he was! "People who love each other don't lie to each other," she said. "The truth is that you were paid to keep me away from Boston and used every trick in the book to do it. No wonder you have so much self-control. It must have been a chore to make love to me every night."

"The only chore was stopping," he said, visibly amused. "You're lucky I'm such an honorable guy."

Jessica didn't answer. She didn't actually believe Griff had had to force himself to touch her, but she didn't believe he loved her, either. She was nothing but an amusing diversion to him, a side benefit to the two-and-a-half grand a week.

Their trailer was just ahead. Jessica would have kept on walking, but Griff took her by the wrist and dragged her to the door. "Give me ten minutes," he said. "Just ten. I might have handled things wrong, but at least give me a chance to explain."

Jessica looked at her watch. "All right, then. You've got till three-twenty."

Fifteen seconds later she was sitting on the sofa while Griff paced back and forth in front of her. In his own mind, he claimed, he'd stopped working for Alex way back in Lake George, when Roxy had told him about Emily's phone call and he'd realized Jessica might be in danger. She heard a great deal about her uncles and cousins and even more about Alex—about his gambling, about his other women, about his questionable acquaintances. Griff insisted that the turning point had come when her cousin Todd had shown up out of nowhere with a friend whose uncle was a member of the mob.

"At that point I decided to change our itinerary." He stopped pacing and sat down beside her. "I'm not letting you out of my sight, Jessica. I don't trust those people."

"What do you think they're going to do? Kidnap me off the street and torture me into voting their way?" Jessica's flippancy concealed a wrenching anguish. It hadn't been easy to listen while people she loved and respected were ripped to shreds. Griff had lied to her so often that she preferred to believe he was still doing it. "I'm lucky I survived my visit with Gail. Todd might have had a hit man on my tail.''

"True," Griff said. "That's why I followed you."

She stared at him, not quite believing it. "But you and Janet—I didn't see her car—"

"I told you before. I spent four years with the FBI—"

"And had all the standard training. I remember." He was good at his job, she had to give him that. "Maybe you think you're telling the truth—I don't know—but *I* think you're being paranoiac. Nobody in my family would harm me. They love me. If they didn't, this whole situation wouldn't be so painful." She looked into her lap, embarrassed by how gullible she'd been and ashamed of what a coward she was. "I should have gone back to Boston last week, but I was too infatuated with you to face up to my responsibilities. Whether I like it or not, my grandparents left me a large block of stock and expected me to do my part in directing the company. I should have demanded a seat on the board and voted my conscience instead of acting like a little child who's afraid people will get mad at her if she says what she really thinks.''

His jaw tightened. "You're not going anywhere, Jessica. I won't let you."

"I don't recall asking your permission," she said coolly. Who did he think he was, her lord and master?

"It wouldn't have mattered if you had," he replied. "I'm not taking you back."

"Then I'll hitch a ride to the ferry and take a bus from Portland." She started to get up, only to be unceremoniously pulled back down. More agitated than ever, she snapped, "I swear, Griff, if you don't let me go, I'll have you arrested for kidnapping. You have no right—"

"I have every right!" he roared at her. "I happen to love you! Maybe you're too naive to understand the danger you might be in, but I'm not. Your uncles run around making crazy threats, your boyfriend pays a fortune to get you out of the way and fills his time with gambling and women while you're gone, your cousin's best buddy has an uncle who's a capo in the Clement family—"

"All of which has nothing to do with my decision," Jessica insisted. "Maybe you're too jaded to care about ethics or morality, but I'm not. Are you going to drive me back to Boston or am I going to get there on my own?"

"Neither." He pulled her onto his lap, so deftly and swiftly that he was holding her in his arms by the time she had the wit to resist. "I'm going to talk some sense into you."

Talk, however, was the last thing he had in mind. The next thing Jessica knew, he was kissing her hard on the lips, thrusting his tongue into her mouth and making love to her with a bold eroticism far more demanding and seductive than anything she'd experienced in the past. For a moment she was too stunned to react. But her emotions were already at flash point, running so high her anger turned to passion with shattering quickness. She didn't even recognize the woman who dug her nails into his shoulders, arched her body against his and kissed him fiercely. Half of her wanted to hit him and half of her wanted to ravish him. She felt like a primordial creature facing something incomprehensible or overwhelming—at the mercy of her instincts and totally out of control.

Griff had been gentle and patient in the past, but now he was fiery and passionate, using his expertise to arouse and overpower her. Jessica felt his hand at her throat, working at the top button of her blouse, and hazily realized how much he must have held back up till now. His body reminded her of a loaded bow—tense and ready to snap.

Everything was happening too fast. He was kissing her hotly and deeply, yanking off her blouse and bra, easing her down until she was lying beneath his body. He wedged his leg between her thighs and began to move against her, his body hard and compelling. She moaned and followed his lead. She felt the soft cotton of his shirt against her breasts, and then, once the shirt was off, his bare chest. His hands came next, caressing and teasing her until her nipples were hard and aching.

Nothing in her life had prepared her to cope with the intensity of her excitement and desire. He kept driving her higher and higher, sliding his mouth to her breasts and sucking roughly and arousingly at the nipples, stroking her intimately and insistently until she longed to feel his hand against her bare skin. By the time he finally unsnapped her shorts and tugged at the side zipper, she knew she wasn't going to stop him. She wanted the same thing he did, but rather than being frightened by that, she was drowning in pure, wild pleasure.

It came as a cold, hard shock when he abruptly pulled away. One moment he was making love to her, searing her with passion, and the next he was standing beside her, breathing rapidly and staring at the wall with glazed eyes. She reached for her blouse and held it against her breasts. Her mind was a blank, her brain too numb to function. Very slowly, she pulled herself up and straightened her back.

He finally looked at her. "I could take you to bed now if I wanted to. You do realize that."

Jessica felt herself redden. Given her upbringing, it was impossible not to be ashamed of the way she'd responded. "So?" she said.

"So you're in love with me. Otherwise you would have stopped me."

"I'm—very attracted to you." The words came out in a whisper. "You must have—you're not—what I'm trying to say—"

"Yes?"

He was smiling now, indulgently and a little smugly. He looked so superior that Jessica forgot about being embarrassed. "You're good at it, that's all! That's all it ever was. You use it to get what you want."

"Ah, I see." He nodded to himself. "It could have been anyone just now, assuming he was good enough in bed, and you would have been willing to sleep with him."

"I didn't say that." Jessica didn't know what she felt. She'd allowed Griff to do as he pleased, but she couldn't love him, not when he'd lied to her from the moment they'd met and had treated her like a simple-minded child. The memories were humiliating enough to stiffen her wilting backbone. "Even if I did love you—which I don't—it wouldn't change anything. I want to go back to Boston."

He cursed under his breath. "If I had any brains, I'd throw you on the bed and keep you there till the fifteenth. It's the one place where you don't give me a hard time."

Jessica wasn't going to dignify his remarks with a response. "I want to go back to Boston," she repeated doggedly.

"Do you know how hard it is for me to stand here without touching you? I try to protect you, I spoil you rotten, I stop myself from taking you to bed because I know you'll feel guilty afterward, and what reward do I get?" He mimicked her tone. "'I want to go back to Boston.' Damn it, Jessica, I have more experience with these types of people than you do. Why won't you listen to me? Don't I deserve a little cooperation?"

Jessica found him maddeningly condescending. "I'm an adult, Griff. I can make my own decisions. I've listened but

I don't agree, and as far as your *reward* goes..." She raised her chin and flung her blouse at his chest. He caught it before it could fall to the ground. "Go ahead, since you're so sure you deserve this. I wouldn't want to owe you anything when we say good-bye in Boston."

"For God's sake, Jessica—"

"No, I mean it, Griff. I wouldn't expect you to torture yourself by denying yourself my body."

He took a deep breath and walked toward her. Jessica's heart began to pound wildly, but he merely draped her blouse around her shoulders and turned away. Then he left the camper, slamming the door behind him.

Chapter Twelve

Griff was crouched in the bushes outside the living room of Charles and Nancy Lawrence's Lincoln home, listening as best he could to the discussion that was taking place inside. Jessica, showing a rare talent for self-destruction, had called the family together and was in the process of announcing her decision regarding the future of Lawrence Shoes. Ernest was openly gleeful while Charles was apoplectic; between the two of them, she was having trouble getting a word in.

Short of tying Jessica to the bed, Griff had had no choice but to take her back to Boston. She'd been hell-bent on leaving, furious with him for being a private investigator, and in no mood to listen to his logic. Since his instincts had told him that arguing would only make her more stubborn, he'd shut his mouth and done as she'd asked. It had never occurred to him that she wouldn't forgive him—she was too softhearted and accommodating to stay angry for long.

The first available ferry had been the Tuesday afternoon boat to Bar Harbor. They'd camped for the night in nearby Ellsworth, arriving at Jessica's at about two the following afternoon. Griff would have preferred to take her to a hotel or his own apartment, but she'd been adamant about picking up her life exactly where she'd left it off. That included him, too—she hadn't wanted to see him or even speak to him again.

After two days of virtual cold war, his confidence had been shaken to the point of half believing her. Desperate for reassurance, he'd made a stiff apology in her hallway, wished her the best of luck in the future, and watched intently for her reaction. He'd been relieved to see her cool facade crack a little—her face had paled and her eyes had filled up. It was just as well that she'd turned and walked away, because otherwise he would have taken her in his arms instead of leaving, thereby getting himself accused all over again of being a womanizing louse who'd manipulated her shamelessly. As hard as it had been to go, he'd realized that nothing could be resolved while she was preoccupied with Lawrence Shoes and confused about her feelings.

He'd been tailing her ever since, spelled by a free-lance operative when he needed to shower or grab a few hours' sleep. At the moment, she was sitting on the edge of an armchair, surrounded by her uncles and their families. Griff had been able to identify everyone by listening and watching. Ernest, Rita, Emily and Ron were all smiles, while Charles was angry and showed it. Nancy looked coldly resentful, Chuck seemed calm to the point of boredom, and Todd was off in a corner sulking. Griff couldn't wait until Friday morning when the Lawrence annual meeting would begin and the firm's fate would be decided. Until then, he was destined to do a lot of worrying and very little sleeping.

Jessica hadn't expected the confrontation with her family to be a picnic, but it was even worse than she'd anticipated. Her Uncle Charles had always had the power to frighten her, but his rage was so extreme she finally turned to her Uncle Ernest and asked if he knew a lawyer she could consult.

A shocked hush fell over the room. "A lawyer? What do you need with a lawyer?" Charles demanded.

"I want to make a will. I'm going to leave my stock to Emily."

Charles glared at her. "Of all the paranoiac, adolescent fantasies—what do you think I'm going to do? Shoot you to keep you away from the meeting?"

"One never knows," Jessica said, outwardly self-assured but inwardly quaking.

"Well, that's crazy. An insult." Charles gestured toward the door. "Go on, get out of here. We might poison your food if you stay."

Jessica hurried to the door, followed within seconds by Ernest. Behind her, she could hear Charles berating his son Todd. "You and your bright ideas! You couldn't leave well enough alone—you had to talk me into letting you try to change her mind. We had a fifty-fifty chance before, but now..." His lecture degenerated into a tirade of abuse.

Ernest walked her to her car, holding an umbrella over her head to protect her from the rain. "Believe me, sweetheart, I know your Uncle Charles better than you do. He's a little upset right now, but he'll calm down. He loves you like his own flesh and blood. He'd never harm you."

"But the things he said—it was so awful..."

"He didn't mean them. He's always been excitable." Ernest opened her car door for her. "Go on home and get some rest. A month and it will all blow over. You'll see."

Jessica wasn't so sure. Maybe she'd been paying too much attention to Griff, but she felt a twinge of apprehension as she started her car. It whined a little at first, but nobody had rigged it to blow up.

She was miserably lonely, lonelier than she'd ever been in her life. She and Griff had spent only three weeks together but it seemed like much longer. She'd missed him every moment they were apart—so much that she'd cried herself to sleep the night before. She tried to tell herself it was a matter of habit rather than love, but you didn't grieve over a man just because you'd gotten used to seeing his face across the table.

She tossed and turned all night, reliving her argument with Charles. Griff had been right about at least one thing— Todd's appearance in North Woodstock hadn't been a coincidence. He'd found out where she was and driven up to see her. More than ever, she began to wonder about Alex's role in the whole incident. The ever-protective Mrs. MacPherson wouldn't have revealed Jessica's whereabouts, so that left Alex. Why had he talked?

For that matter, why had he asked her to marry him? Why had he paid thousands of dollars to get her out of town? Because he loved her and wanted to protect her, or because he was scheming to get his hands on her money?

She'd always thought he had plenty of money of his own, but gambling and women were expensive vices. Had he realized even sooner than she that her conscience and heart were with Ernest and that she would vote his way if she attended the annual meeting? Certainly he'd known her stock was worth a small fortune if the company was sold but almost nothing otherwise. Perhaps he'd decided to get her out of Boston for the meeting and marry her as soon as possible if the vote went Charles's way. It never would have occurred to her to question Alex's handling of their finances if he'd actually become her husband. She'd seen him as far more knowledgeable about such matters than she was.

She awoke the next morning with a throbbing headache and such a twisting sense of loss that not even her beloved flute could ease it. Nobody really cared about her—they only pretended to because they wanted something from her. Certainly that was true of Alex and her family, and as for Griff, his good-bye had been shockingly final.

She stared at the phone. Only a dope would have expected him to call. He'd said and done everything in his power to fulfill his agreement with Alex, but then, when she'd found him out, washed his hands of the whole affair. He hadn't even given her his private phone number so she could call him if she changed her mind about seeing him. So much for his fears about her safety and his protestations of love!

Then again, she hadn't exactly encouraged him. She'd accused him of using sex to manipulate her, or at least of amusing himself with her body. She'd told him not to call her or come to her house. She'd even turned her back on his final attempt to apologize. Maybe the next move was up to her.

She thought about phoning his office, but couldn't bring herself to take the risk. How could she fathom his true feelings when she hadn't even known who he was until three days before? Besides, he'd been so cool at the end. He hadn't given any sign that he cared for her.

It rained all day Thursday, heavily and unrelentingly. Jessica went out only once, to see a lawyer she'd picked out of a phone book. For a modest fee, he drafted a will leaving her stock to Emily and everything else to Mrs. Mac-Pherson. The sole exception was her flute. In a gesture that was as quixotic as it was sentimental, she willed the instrument to Griff. He'd lied about a lot of things, but not about loving the way she played. She was sure of that.

She dropped a copy of the will in her safety deposit box on her way home and then shut herself into her house. After practicing for a couple of hours, she picked at some lunch, practiced a little more and watched an old movie on TV. The film, a murder mystery containing a scene where the victim's will was destroyed, prompted her to call her uncles and tell them what she'd done. Ernest insisted she was being silly while Charles cursed under his breath and hung up on her.

By late afternoon she was stir-crazy. She'd never known you could be restless and depressed at the same time. When the doorbell rang she rushed to see who it was. Any interruption would have been welcome by then, even the Fuller Brush man.

It wasn't a salesman outside, but her cousin Todd. Not trusting him, Jessica poked her head out the door and said, "I'm not going to change my mind. You're wasting your time."

He hung his head in remorse. "I'm scum, Jessica, stagnant pond scum. How can I apologize?"

"You just did. If that's all you want—"

He wedged his foot in the door and grinned at her, suddenly the old Todd again. "I'm here to make it up to you. How about a movie and dinner?" He named a comedy she'd been dying to see and a restaurant she absolutely loved. It was out on the south shore, so she seldom drove down to eat there. "No strings, Jessie Lynn," he promised. "I'll be good, I swear it."

Suspicious, Jessica said, "Your credibility is a little low right now. Why don't you tell me what you *really* want?"

"Hell, Jessica, we were always pals. Other than me, you're the only sane one in the family. I don't like having you mad at me."

That was typical of Todd. He wanted people to like him even when he'd been thoughtless or selfish. Jessica hadn't forgiven him yet, but his smile was so winning she softened. Why send him away when she was lonely and bored?

"All right, then," she said, "but we're taking my car. One word about Lawrence Shoes and you can walk home."

"Right," he agreed. "Absolutely."

He was as good as his word, telling her about his latest romance on the way to the movies and talking about college as they drove to the restaurant. Jessica was in a much better mood by then—the film had more than lived up to its good reviews. By the time they finished dinner, she was charitable enough toward Todd to take care of the check. His summer job with the shoe company paid only minimum wage, so he was perpetually broke.

She stifled a yawn as they walked to the car. She'd slept very little these past two nights, and it had finally caught up with her. If Todd hadn't had so much to drink, she would have asked him to drive home.

It was quite late out and the night was very dark. Jessica drove slowly and cautiously—the road from the shore to the highway was narrow and curvy. Todd was quiet for once, so she switched on the radio for company. Handel's *Water Music* was playing.

A car was behind her, waiting to pass, so she slowed down and moved to her right. It sped by at the first opportunity and disappeared around a curve. Jessica was humming along with the music, relaxed for the first time in days. When she reached the curve and saw a set of taillights, she slowed a little more. Then, without warning, the car in front of her swerved, squealed, and came to a dead stop across both lanes of the road. She had to slam on her brakes to avoid hitting it.

Todd opened his door and started to get out. "Something must be wrong there. I'll see if we can help."

He was walking toward the jackknifed car when the doors swung open and two men got out. Time seemed to slow down. Todd began to back away, but the men charged to either side of him and grabbed him before he could get away. Jessica caught the glint of light on metal—both of them had guns. She locked the car, then froze. One of the men had ended Todd's struggles with a sharp blow from his gun.

It took Jessica several precious seconds to realize that it was pointless to stick around; her only chance was to abandon Todd and go for help. By the time she restarted her engine, the second man had run to her car, smashed her window with his gun and pulled up the lock. He opened her door as she put the car in drive, grabbing her arm before she could press the accelerator. She fought as hard as she could, but he was much too strong for her. Just looking at him was enough to make her shake—he had a black stocking over his head, like some ghoulish executioner.

Fighting down hysteria, she asked him what he wanted. "If it's money—"

"You'd better pray your family's willing to pay it." He picked her up and tossed her over his shoulder. Jessica could tell he was trying not to hurt her, but she was still completely terrified. This wasn't a random attack—these men must have been following her and Todd since Boston, only waiting until it was dark to make their move.

Her abductor dumped her in the back of the car and joined his partner in front. Todd was in the back, too, woozy but conscious, guarded by the barrel of a gun. Jessica was almost too scared to breathe. The driver gunned the gas, cut to his left and sped off down the road.

* * *

Griff followed from a safe distance, debating his options. Given the guns and the size of the men, an out-and-out attack was pointless. He'd have to bide his time and wait for an opening.

He tailed them for about thirty miles, until they pulled into a driveway off an isolated back road. By the time he parked his car and trotted to the house, everyone was inside. He could see into the front hall through a crack between the curtains, but it was empty. About five minutes later the two men came down the stairs, minus their masks now. Griff didn't recognize the first, but the second was Sonny Petronelli.

He crouched by the window, weighing his alternatives. Should he launch a surprise attack? Attempt a clandestine rescue? Either might work, but both carried the risk of violence. Maybe there was a better way—a way that would reveal exactly what was going on here and knock some sense into the woman he loved at the same time.

Jessica knew she'd been a fool. It wasn't as if Griff hadn't warned her, so why hadn't she listened instead of insisting her family would act rationally? When had she become so stubborn, so unreasonable, so all-fired stupid?

Despite her abductor's remarks, she was sure this was no ordinary kidnapping. One of her uncles had to be behind it, probably Charles, because he only had a chance to win if he kept her away from tomorrow's meeting. If Charles had hired these men, she was relatively safe. Her absence was as good as her death, so why go to the trouble of killing her?

And if Ernest had hired them? How did she know what demons might have come to haunt him in the middle of the night? Maybe he'd decided she would change her mind and not show up, that Charles would win after all. Her death would assure him of victory because Emily would get to vote her stock. The possibility made Jessica's blood run cold.

She and Todd were gagged with scarves and tied to chairs on opposite sides of a pitch-black bedroom. She could hear him struggling to escape but doubted he'd succeed. The ropes had been tied by experts.

Eventually exhaustion overtook her and she dozed off. She woke with a panicky start, saw moonlight falling on the window shades, and squinted at Todd. He was quiet and still—everything in the house seemed to be.

She began to long for Griff so fiercely that her chest got tight and her eyes began to burn. It wasn't that he might have been able to protect her if they'd been together during the attack, but that she might never see him again. She was twice a fool. She hadn't listened to his fears for her safety and she hadn't listened to her own heart. Her anger and humiliation had blinded her.

Now, faced with the possibility of her own death, she realized how dearly her pride had cost her. She'd been crazy about Griff almost from the beginning and still was. If only she could turn back the clock and react differently—but she couldn't.

She called out to Todd but got no answer. Her joints were stiff and sore by now, but wiggling in her chair did little to relieve the ache. Panic began to rise in her throat when she thought about what might happen, but she kept it in check by telling herself they would have killed her already if that had been their intention.

Some time later—it could have been fifteen minutes and it could have been an hour—she heard a loud, insistent knocking on the front door. Her fears grew almost uncontrollable. Why would somebody show up in the middle of the night unless it was to kill her? She started to struggle frantically, but the ropes held firm.

A thin, bright strip appeared at the bottom of her door—somebody had turned on the lights in the hall. The sound of footfalls followed, first in the hallway and then on the stairs. Jessica's heart was beating wildly now. The front door had just opened. People were talking, but she couldn't make out what they were saying.

She heard the click of shoes on the steps—lots of shoes, not just the one pair of slippers. She was numb with horror as they approached the door, her mind a total blank.

She blinked against the sudden brightness as the door swung open. All she could see were silhouettes. Then somebody turned on the overhead light and she recognized Griff. She went limp with relief, her body shaking in reaction. As he rushed to her side, tears began to stream down her cheeks.

He took out a knife and cut away her gag, then gathered her into his arms. She buried her face against his shoulder and sobbed out her feelings. "I was so scared. I thought I'd never see you again. I love you so much."

"It's okay. Everything's going to be okay." He drew away a little and pulled out a tissue, dabbing at her eyes. "Let me get these ropes off, sweetheart."

Jessica slowly got a grip on herself as he worked on the ropes. On the other side of the room, somebody was freeing Todd—Sonny Petronelli, she realized. Two other men were standing in the doorway, but she didn't recognize either of them. One was young and huge—one of her abductors, she assumed—and the other was gray-haired and slight. He reminded her of her grandfather.

The older man gave a courtly nod. "My apologies, Miss Lawrence."

Jessica stared at him. "Who are you?"

"A friend of Mr. Marshall's." He smiled ironically. "Let's go downstairs. Certain matters need to be cleared up."

Todd, Jessica noticed, had turned a sickly shade of gray. Sonny didn't look much better, and neither did his friend. The old man with Griff might have seemed harmless, but obviously he scared the wits out of these people.

Down in the living room, Griff settled her on the couch and sat down beside her. "How are you doing?" he asked.

"Okay." She didn't understand what was going on here. "Griff, that man with you—"

"Don't ask questions," he interrupted softly. "Your curiosity's gotten you into enough trouble already."

The old man took a seat, but Todd, Sonny and Sonny's friend remained standing. "So? Who paid for this?" he demanded, openly contemptuous of the three of them.

Sonny pointed to Todd. "He did. I got Ralph to help us. Todd's my friend, Uncle Carlo. I wanted to do him a favor. We weren't going to hurt her."

Carlo ignored that. "And who paid *you*?" he asked Todd.

Todd was silent for a long, tense moment, until Sonny said through gritted teeth, "Damn it, don't you realize who he is? Answer him!"

Todd shifted his feet uneasily. "A guy named Alex Ulanoff. We ran into each other at a private club the other night and I mentioned Jessica was back—that she intended to vote against selling Lawrence Shoes. He was very upset by that. His reaction surprised me, but then I put two and two together. No offense, Jessica, but your stock was probably a big part of your attraction. Alex wanted to marry you because he figured he could get his hands on a fortune—but only if the sale went through. That's why he was willing to tell me you were in North Woodstock—because he knew I wanted to try and talk you into selling."

"Ah, yes, Ulanoff. The theater director." Carlo smiled and nodded. "I'm not surprised he would be interested in money. I hear he's a heavy gambler. Losses in six figures, not that I would know anything personally."

"Of course not," Griff agreed, and then asked Todd, "And your father? Did he have anything to do with it?"

Todd shook his head. "I was only going to tell him if it worked. He's been on my case for months, threatening to cut me off if I got into any more trouble, and meeting Ulanoff seemed like a golden opportunity. I had a feeling he'd be willing to pay to have Jessica removed, and I was right. He bit the moment I suggested it. It was supposed to look like a kidnap for ransom—Jessica would turn up missing and Alex would find out where she was and rescue her. Sonny and Ralph would escape and never be found." He shrugged. "I needed money to pay off my debts. I figured Dad would be grateful if I got Jessica out of the way— that he'd stop ragging on me. He's a little too straight to have thought of this himself, but he wouldn't object to the outcome—not as long as his hands stayed clean."

Griff shook his head in disgust and turned to Carlo. "I don't want Ulanoff or anyone else to know Jessica is free. It would be best if these three gentlemen stayed here until tomorrow at ten, when the meeting begins."

Carlo nodded. "They'll stay. No phone calls, Sonny." He slowly got up. "Now, Mr. Marshall, if you don't mind, I'm an old man. I need my sleep."

Jessica walked out of the house in a dreamlike fog. Had Alex actually paid to have her kidnapped? And this Carlo person—was he actually what he seemed? If so, how did Griff know such a man, much less ask him for favors? And how had he found out she was in trouble in the first place?

Griff settled her in the back of his car, covering her with a wool blanket. "Try to get some sleep. We'll talk later."

As he straightened, Jessica threw her arms around his neck in agitation. "Griff—"

"I know. It's been a tough couple of days." He kissed her on the forehead and tucked her arms back under the cover. "For once in your life, do as you're told. Okay?"

Jessica swallowed hard. It hadn't escaped her that she'd told Griff she loved him but hadn't heard the same thing back. Obviously he was annoyed with her, and why not? She'd caused him a great deal of trouble. "Anything you say," she answered meekly.

"Such submissiveness," he said with a grin. "It should only last."

Jessica turned onto her side. She was so tired that the silence and gentle motion of the car soon lulled her to sleep. She finally woke when they came to a stop. Pulling herself up, she saw that Carlo's door was open. She gave a sniff. The air was heavy with salt. She could make out a house about twenty feet away.

Carlo was still in front, shaking Griff's hand. "We're even now, Mr. Marshall. Yes?"

"Yes," Griff agreed.

Carlo laughed softly. "I'll tell you a secret. You could have come to me, anyway, about your fiancée. It's a very bad thing to have one's subordinates involved in independent operations. It undermines one's authority."

"I'll keep that in mind," Griff said. "Good-night."

Fiancée? Jessica wondered if Griff had really meant it, or had only told Carlo they were engaged to enlist his cooperation. She yawned and sat up.

"So you're awake," Griff said once they were alone in the car. "Come up front. I want to ask you something."

Jessica obediently·joined him, worrying about what he planned to say. He tucked his finger under her chin to raise it, bringing his mouth so close to her face that she could feel his breath on her skin. "What was all that about loving me?" he murmured. "Panic? Gratitude?"

Jessica started to tremble. Everything would be out in the open now. If he rejected her, she was going to curl up and die. "I love you, that's all. I've missed you so much—when you hold me this way—I just—I can't—" She had too big a lump in her throat to continue.

"I see." He was smiling crookedly now. "Does that mean I'm forgiven for lying to you?"

"You know you are," Jessica whispered.

He brushed his lips across her mouth. The kiss was velvet-soft, but it affected Jessica like a raging bonfire. She needed to be in Griff's arms, needed the reassurance of his lovemaking. She pressed herself as close as she could get and tasted his lips with her tongue. Within moments they were sharing a deep, intense kiss. Jessica felt as if she would never be able to get enough of him. She wanted to crawl inside his skin and become a physical part of him.

She was shaking with desire by the time he eased her away. "There are better places to seduce you than in the local godfather's driveway," he said hoarsely.

"You don't have to seduce me," Jessica replied. "Take me home to your bed. Make love to me tonight."

"Best offer I've had in years." Griff was smiling as he straightened and started the car. "I owe Ulanoff a lot. If he hadn't paid Todd to kidnap you, it might have taken you weeks to come to your senses and figure out you loved me."

Jessica rolled her eyes. "If you're trying to get a rise out of me by being arrogant—"

"Who's being arrogant? I'm stating facts." He gave her a quick, hard kiss before pulling out. "Here's another one.

I love you like crazy. Now let's go home and get some sleep."

"Sleep?" Jessica repeated, teasing him.

"Sleep," he repeated firmly. "I've been tailing you for the past two days—sleeping in my car, crawling around in thorny bushes, getting soaked to the skin. I'm exhausted."

Jessica doubted he was *that* exhausted. He was simply acting the gentleman again, protecting her from her own emotions. A part of her was disappointed, but she also felt a wave of relief. She wasn't the type for an affair, and it was a little early in the game to talk about getting married.

As they drove back to Boston, he told her about Carlo Clement, the singularly dangerous man who headed the family that bore his name. "I met him about six years ago. An FBI informant was doing business with him inside this same beach house—it's his summer place. The informant was wearing a wire, and I was out on the road recording the conversation. The informant was just about to leave when a woman's voice came over my receiver, hysterical. I heard something about a baby wandering into the ocean—that they'd pulled her out but she wasn't breathing. Clement rushed to call an ambulance, but you've seen where he lives. There isn't a hospital within fifteen or twenty miles. The little girl could have died by the time anybody came. I knew C.P.R. I couldn't just sit there and do nothing."

"So you went inside and gave her artificial respiration?"

Griff nodded. "She turned out to be Clement's favorite grandchild. He was so grateful he wanted to set me up in business, but of course I refused. Meanwhile, my superiors were furious with me. I'd compromised the identity of an informant and screwed up an investigation. After that, I more or less stuck to computers."

"And the informant? Was he, uh—"

"No. He testified at several trials and then went into the federal witness protection program. We never did nail Clement, but we got some of the people in his organization."

Jessica understood everything now. "So you followed me after I was grabbed out of my car, recognized Sonny Petronelli, and went to Clement for help. He owed you a favor."

"Right. He was glad to pay me back, especially when I told him I'd left the FBI." Griff gave a laugh. "He even offered me another job—as his personal private investigator. Said I wouldn't have to break the law if I didn't want to. I'll tell you, I could be a rich guy if I were willing to work for crooks."

"You wouldn't be the man I love if you were willing to work for crooks." Relaxed and happy, Jessica leaned against Griff's shoulder and closed her eyes. Life was ironic. Alex had tried to maneuver her into marrying him and unwittingly thrown her together with the most terrific man in the world. She would have to thank him for that when she saw him.

Chapter Thirteen

Somehow Jessica wasn't surprised that the opportunity to thank Alex should arrive the very next morning at the Lawrence annual meeting. Given his keen interest in the outcome, it was only logical that he would show up.

Dozens of stockholders and employees were milling around the conference room and corridor when she and Griff walked in, drinking coffee and talking. Charles spotted her almost at once, Ernest half a minute later. Neither seemed surprised to see her. Alex came striding down the hall soon afterward, just as people were drifting to their seats. The bland expression on his face turned to shock when he noticed Jessica, but only for a split second. If she hadn't been looking his way, she never would have seen the telltale guilt in his eyes.

He continued over to them, as confident and cheerful as ever, and gave Jessica a peck on the cheek. "You're looking wonderful, darling. Why didn't you tell me you were back?"

"I didn't have to," Jessica replied. "Todd did it for me."
She opened her purse and took out his ring. "I'm sure you'll
want to return this. From what I hear, you can use the
money."

Griff put a possessive arm around Jessica's shoulders as
Alex shoved the ring in his pocket. The message was unmistakable—he was announcing that they belonged together. Alex must have realized he was beaten because his
eyes narrowed and he backed away.

Then he smiled coldly. "I suppose you've told her everything, Marshall. Having you pretend to be your father was
a brilliant idea, except for one thing. You're young and
handsome. Disguised or not, you were bound to attract her
eventually, and since propinquity has a way of leading to
lust, it's not surprising that you took advantage of her."

Jessica felt Griff tense up. "As a matter of fact, I didn't,
but I don't think we need to continue this conversation. If
you'll excuse us—"

"I have to talk to you, Jessica. Please—wait a minute."
Alex's cynical facade crumbled abruptly. In all the years
Jessica had known him, she'd never seen such panic in his
eyes. She wondered if it was real, or only another act. "I did
love you," he said to her. "I was good to you and your
grandparents, wasn't I?"

"Only because they made large donations to your theater company while they were alive and because you figured you could marry Jessica once they were gone and live
off her inheritance," Griff replied. "What did you do?
Gamble away your trust fund?" When Alex didn't answer
right away, he went on angrily, "You and your damn fool
plots! Do you have any idea how terrified she was last night?
Do you even care?"

"But they promised they wouldn't hurt her," Alex insisted. "I would have rescued her and she would have been

grateful. Then she would have done whatever I asked her to. It all would have worked out—except for you." Much to her chagrin, Jessica realized she'd once been gullible enough to believe what he'd wanted her to, and perhaps even docile enough to react the way he'd expected.

He gave her a pleading look. "Think about everything I did for you—all the times you cried on my shoulder, all the evenings I spent entertaining your grandparents. I gamble, Jessica. It's a sickness—I want to stop but I can't. When the trust fund was gone, I tried to recoup my losses by using money donated to N.E.T.C. I borrowed nearly a quarter of a million dollars and lost it all. If I don't replace it by the year-end audit, I could go to jail. I spoke to my father but he refuses to help. You're the only one I can turn to. You've got to sell Lawrence Shoes and lend me the money I need."

Jessica was stunned. How could a man as bright as Alex also be so weak and foolish? It was so pathetic, so degrading, that she couldn't bring herself to be angry with him. With the meeting due to start any minute, she didn't have time to analyze or debate, so her emotions did the answering. "You're asking me to go against my upbringing and my conscience, Alex. I can't do that. I won't vote to sell. But however else I can help you, I will. Please, just leave now. I'll call you Monday morning, once I've had a chance to think things over."

He didn't move. "I'm begging you, Jessica. Please, you've got to get me the money. I don't want to go to jail. I'll get treatment. I'll do anything you want."

"The lady just told you what she wants," Griff said. "Let's leave it at that, shall we?"

Despite Griff's mild tone, there was a coldness in his eyes and a coiled energy in his body that bespoke real menace. Alex seemed to sense the danger because he straightened, nodded and walked away. Jessica watched him hurry down the hall, then entered the meeting room and sat down. She was grateful that Griff was by her side. His presence gave her confidence and strength.

Reports were given, decisions were made, and ballots were distributed. As soon as the vote had been tallied, Ernest read out the results. Had Jessica abstained, Charles would have won, but of course, he hadn't. He looked so coldly furious that Jessica assumed it would be the end of their relationship.

She approached the table slowly, steeling herself for a tirade. Charles was gathering together his papers while Ernest sat savoring his victory. He grabbed Jessica's shoulders and gave her a triumphant little shake. "We'll have to get you on the board now. It's time we had a woman to replace your grandmother."

Jessica told him she would think it over, and introduced him to Griff. Charles, meanwhile, had stopped fiddling with his papers and was watching the three of them intently. At the first opportunity, he held out his hand to Griff. "Charles Lawrence," he said. "You're the sociologist, I take it."

Griff smiled. "His son, actually. It's a long story."

Charles looked from Griff to Jessica and back again, taking in the way Griff's arm was draped around her shoulders. "You'll have to bring him to dinner some night," he said to his niece.

"If you'd like us to come, of course we will," Jessica replied.

"You're family. We own a business together. We have to deal with each other." Charles shoved his papers into a leather portfolio and smiled brittlely. "Who knows? Perhaps my brother will become so successful now that he owns Fabrini Footwear that he'll be able to buy me out." He stood up and stalked out of the room.

Jessica declined Ernest's invitation to attend a victory luncheon and left with Griff. It was such a lovely day that they decided to go on a picnic. An hour later they were sitting on a blanket in the park near Griff's apartment, eating salads and cold cuts out of paper containers.

They hadn't talked about anything more serious than what to buy and where to go, but Griff finally raised the subject that was on both of their minds. "What are you going to do about Ulanoff? A quarter of a million bucks is a lot of money."

"I could raise it if I sold the house, but I couldn't bring myself to do that," Jessica said.

Griff smiled. "The Lawrence family legacy, I suppose."

"Not really." Jessica reddened a little. They hadn't discussed the future yet, so she had no way of knowing if Griff had thought about getting married. "I already think of it as *our* house. Your apartment is awfully small, not that I wouldn't live there if you wanted me to."

"You think I'd prefer a one-bedroom rental to a four-bedroom house that's bought and paid for?" Griff shook his head, laughing. "No way, sweetheart. We'll live in the house."

"My grandmother used to say that men could be proud."

"Proud, yes. Stupid, no." Griff paused, then rushed ahead. "Look, Jessica, I know this is none of my business, but I have to say what I think. There's no reason you should bail Ulanoff out. Everything he did for you and your grandparents, he did from the most selfish motives imaginable. It's bad enough that he hired me to get you out of town—he was even willing to stage a phony kidnapping and rescue, just so you'd be grateful and do what he wanted. The worst that will probably happen is that he'll get convicted of embezzlement and shipped to a minimum security prison. He'll probably spend the time writing his autobiography and wind up earning a fortune in royalties. Believe me, the guy will land on his feet. His kind always does."

Jessica couldn't argue with what he'd said because all of it was probably true. Somehow, though, the truth wasn't the issue here. "Whatever his motives, he was there when I needed someone. He was good to me, Griff. I feel I should repay him. I've got some jewelry I could sell, and there's also what's left in my trust fund. At least it's a start—maybe it would be enough to keep him out of jail if he can work out a schedule to repay the rest of it."

"You realize you'll never get it back."

"Probably not," Jessica agreed.

"And you realize that I don't like it. It bothers me that you'd do this for some other guy."

Jessica broke into an impish smile. "But he got us together, Griff. Why don't you look at it as a sort of finder's fee?"

Griff laughed and pulled her onto his lap. "I guess I can't object, not when your generosity is one of the things I love about you." He took her face in his hands, teased apart her lips, and kissed her slowly and thoroughly. Every time he touched her, she was quicker to catch fire. Within moments, the rest of the world had faded away.

She hazily thought of the night before. If Griff had been exhausted, she couldn't wait to see what he'd be like when he was full of energy. He'd kissed her and touched her until she was moaning in his arms, then given her the most shattering pleasure she'd ever known. She realized there was a lot left to learn and experience, but she couldn't crave what she'd never had. She'd been blissfully content when she'd finally gone to bed.

For Griff, though, it had been different. He hadn't said so, but it was obvious that anything short of real lovemaking was intensely frustrating to him. If he'd waited, it was only because he knew she preferred it.

He finally seemed to remember they were in a public park and buried his lips against her neck. "I never should have started this," he muttered. "It's too tough to stop."

Jessica answered in a husky, teasing voice. "Just as long as you're not asking me to sleep with you. I seem to remember something about not doing that until we know each other better."

He groaned aloud. "It was a line, Jessica. You would have taken off for Boston if I hadn't said that. The truth is, a few more nights like the last one, and—" He cut himself off, grimacing.

"Yes?" Jessica prompted.

"And I'm going to take you to bed," he finally finished. "I don't have the willpower to keep stopping myself and both of us know you won't, either. You're too crazy about me."

Jessica suppressed a chuckle. "It's amazing, but I'm beginning to find your arrogance endearing." She sighed heavily. "We'll have to get married, Griff—there's no alternative. Of course, we'll want to wait a few months, until we know each other better and everyone in the family's on speaking terms again. It's just as well, because I'll have more time to make arrangements that way. We can hold the reception at Uncle Ernest's country club—it's beautiful in the fall. The only problem is that I've gotten used to having you around, but I suppose you could use my guest room. With Mrs. MacPherson there to chaperon, nobody could possibly say a word."

He frowned at her. "If you think I'm going to spend another couple of months sleeping down the hall from you without taking you to bed, you're crazy."

"But there's no choice," Jessica said helplessly. "You can't expect me to live in sin."

Maybe it was Jessica's wide-eyed look and maybe it was her ingenuous tone, but Griff finally realized he was being teased. "Fish or cut bait, lady. Either we get married as soon as possible or we live in what you so quaintly referred to as a state of sin. Personally I'd prefer the first. I'd just as soon not have to cope with your battle-ax of a housekeeper looking at me as if I were some sort of sex maniac."

Jessica did her best to sound resigned. "Then I have no choice. I'll have to marry you now and get to know you afterward." She reached into her purse and pulled out a gold ring, the one he'd bought her in Holyoke. "Who would have thought I'd be wearing this for real some day?"

Griff laughed and offered to buy her a fancier one, but she wouldn't hear of it. The ring reminded her of how they'd met. She would wear it for the rest of her life.

She handed it to Griff, who slid it onto her finger and took her in his arms. "It's amazing how married I feel," she whispered coyly. "Your apartment *is* just across the street, darling."

He didn't need a second invitation.

*   *   *   *   *

Silhouette Romance

This month, some of your all-time favorites have returned to their "alma mater." Next month, some of the continuing stars of the Silhouette Romance line join in the celebration. Don't miss it—come home to Romance.

"Homecoming Celebration"

COMING NEXT MONTH

#532 WOMAN HATER—Diana Palmer
To Nicky White, rugged Montana rancher Winthrop Christopher was irresistible. But he wasn't moved by her charms. Could Nicky convince a confirmed woman hater to love again?

#533 MYSTERY LOVER—Annette Broadrick
Some men send flowers, some send cards, but Chad sent his thoughts—by telepathy. Jennifer loved him, but would she ever see her mystery lover face to face?

#534 THE WINTER HEART—Victoria Glenn
Actress Amanda Ryan was dedicated to her work—and to raising her sister's orphaned child. Then she met unfeeling Brad Winter—her niece's uncle. Could Amanda bring warmth to Brad's winter heart?

#535 GENTLE PERSUASION—Rita Rainville
Even though Kaylie West was the only witness to a robbery, she wasn't worried. But ex-Green Beret Adam Masters knew he had to keep her safe—even if he spent the rest of their lives doing it....

#536 OUTBACK NIGHTS—Emilie Richards
Model Rusty Ames was tired of the rat race; Australia was about as far from New York as she could get. But would a trip into the outback with devilish Aussie Daniel Marlin change her life forever?

#537 FAR FROM OVER—Brittany Young
When dignified lawyer Pierce Westcott met impulsive private eye Samantha English, he had no idea what he was in for. She had a knack for trouble, not at all the kind of woman he'd want for a wife—or was she?

ATTRACTIVE, SPACE SAVING BOOK RACK

Display your most prized novels on this handsome and sturdy book rack. The hand-rubbed walnut finish will blend into your library decor with quiet elegance, providing a practical organizer for your favorite hard-or soft-covered books.

Only $9.95

Approximately 16" x 8" when assembled

Assembles in seconds!

To order, rush your name, address and zip code, along with a check or money order for $10.70* ($9.95 plus 75¢ postage and handling) payable to *Silhouette Books.*

Silhouette Books
Book Rack Offer
901 Fuhrmann Blvd.
P.O. Box 1396
Buffalo, NY 14269-1396

Offer not available in Canada.

BKR-2A

*New York and Iowa residents add appropriate sales tax.

Starting in October...

SHADOWS ON THE NILE

by

Heather Graham Pozzessere

A romantic short story in six installments from best-selling author Heather Graham Pozzessere.

The first chapter of this intriguing romance will appear in all Silhouette titles published in October. The remaining five chapters will appear, one per month, in Silhouette Intimate Moments' titles for November through March '88.

Don't miss "*Shadows on the Nile*"—a special treat, coming to you in October. Only from Silhouette Books.

Be There!

IMSS-1